KU-531-614

Dead Man Walking

Young Nelson is more than a little surprised when he receives a letter from his dying uncle who claims to have secreted a fortune in gold in Bronco Canyon, Arizona. Eager to take advantage of this unexpected windfall, he secures a job as a muleskinner with a wagon train heading west.

But fate steps in with an unexpected twist in the form of a ghost from the past. Who is the mysterious predator also claiming a right to the loot? Will he succeed in thwarting Nelson's plan for a new life with the lovely Emma Driscoll?

A final bloody showdown will settle the matter once and for all.

Writing as Dale Graham

High Plains Vendetta
Dance with the Devil
Nugget!
Montezuma's Legacy
Death Rides Alone
Gambler's Dawn
Vengeance at Bittersweet
Justice for Crockett
Bluecoat Renegade

Dead Man Walking

Ethan Flagg

A Black Horse Western

ROBERT HALE · LONDON

© Ethan Flagg 2008
First published in Great Britain 2008

ISBN 978-0-7090-8509-6

Robert Hale Limited
Clerkenwell House
Clerkenwell Green
London EC1R 0HT

www.halebooks.com

The right of Ethan Flagg to be identified as
author of this work has been asserted by him
in accordance with the Copyright, Designs and
Patents Act 1988

MORAY COUNCIL LIBRARIES & INFO.SERVICES	
20 23 87 03	
Askews	
WF	

Typeset by
Derek Doyle & Associates, Shaw Heath
Printed and bound in Great Britain by
Antony Rowe Limited, Wiltshire

ONE

PECOS FERRY

It was early evening. A young muleskinner was leaning against the stern rail of the river ferry. Casually he pushed back his wide-brimmed slouch hat and took a pull on the newly rolled stogie, allowing the blue smoke to be whipped away by a freshening breeze. Beneath his feet he could feel the ferry dipping and straining as it was pulled across the narrows of the Pecos River in New Mexico territory.

The convoy of twenty-five freight wagons had been forced to make a substantial detour to reach Conchas, one of the few crossing points available at this time of year. Following the spring floods, the river level was particularly high.

They had arrived just before noon. And with only two wagons able to make the crossing at any one time, it was a long-drawn-out process. A pensive cast creased the youthful contours as the smoker cast a languid eye towards the western horizon.

This was the time of day he loved best. The sun, dipping easily as it hung low in the purpling sky, was reflected in the placid calm of the swirling waters like a golden carpet. He peered down at the ripples fanning out from the blunt stern – white lips of surf that kissed each other before dissolving. A loose smile played across the sun-bronzed features as he watched a flock of meadowlarks play chase with each other.

But life had not always been so idyllic.

He recalled the rogue dust storm that had battered the wagons whilst crossing Indian territory. Then there was the attack by a band of Comanche renegades. Luckily the stock of new Springfield rifles due for delivery to the army depot at Santa Fe had proved more than a match for the redskins.

And if that wasn't enough, there was the ever-present daily grind.

Soft blistered hands had long since become hardened by months of gruelling toil: the pale insipid complexion burnished to a deep bronze beneath the blistering sun. And the slack-muscled body of a pen-pusher was now that of a rangy muleskinner.

Maybe it was seeing the end in sight that had given the journey a rose-tinted image. They had been on the trail for almost two months. With only a couple of brief stopovers at isolated trading posts to take on fresh supplies, it had been a long trek. Another week should see them unloading the wagons in the frontier boom town of Santa Fe.

Thoughts of what lay beyond that celebrated gateway to the west propelled a cold tremor of anticipation down the young man's spine.

Gingerly. his hand slid inside the serge jacket, there to fondle the envelope containing those all-important documents. Throughout the entire trek they had never once left his person.

Not long now.

Eyes brown as seasoned mahogany softened and a dreamy expression suffused the young muleskinner's weathered features. Soon he would be able to learn the truth regarding his uncle's legacy. And what that distant canyon on Arizona's Natanes Plateau concealed.

It had all started back in Leavenworth, Kansas where he was employed by the Sovereign Freight Line in the capacity of a lowly inventory clerk.

The letter had arrived in an official envelope postmarked Flagstaff, Arizona. Inside was another envelope, much stained and dog-eared. It was the contents of this that had so excited the young man. Written in a barely legible hand, it also contained a hand-drawn map. After much deliberation, he had managed to decipher the following message:

Dear Nephew,
I am writing this from my hospital bed in Flagstaff. You are my only remaining kin following the early death of your dear mother Elizabeth from the cholera. So it is to you that I entrust the whereabouts of my discovery. The enclosed map gives the details of where a heap of gold nuggets have been stashed. My partner tried to double cross me by sticking a shiv in my guts.

He got a belly full of hot lead for his trouble. The sawbones tells me that I'll pull through. But I know different. Bin here afore. So its up to you now.
  Good luck. Your uncle, Jeb Stockwell.

PS. By the time you read this I'll be pushing up the daisies. Watch out for carpetbaggers. Arizona is full of them. If you don't own a gun, then get one and learn how to use it.

The opportunity for adventure had always beckoned invitingly. Many were the hours that the young clerk had spent at his desk, dreaming of emulating the intrepid journeys of the pioneers who had struck out into the wild uncharted territories of the American West. Men with magical names such as Kit Carson and Jim Bridger who had turned their dreams into reality. But it all took guts and a resolute determination to face down hidden dangers.

Thus far the will to throw over the security of regular work and the comforts afforded by city life had precluded any such display of reckless abandon.

This letter and the challenge it offered was the booster he needed. The chance to make a fresh start, and come out the other end set up for life. Unfortunately, he had little in the way of savings. The wages of a humble clerk had seen to that. There was no way he could afford to pay for a long journey west.

But there was another way. Being employed by a freight line had its advantages. He could sign on as a muleskinner and work his passage.

*

'Penny for them!'

The broad Irish lilt startled the young man out of his musings. 'Or should I be saying a nickel.' Mick Riley chuckled at his own wit. He also was avidly looking forward to reaching trail's end, but more for the chance to sample the fleshpots of Santa Fe.

'Just thinking,' murmured the young man.

He didn't elaborate. Although he had become friendly with the bluff Irishman early on during the trip, his purpose in making it had remained a secret. It didn't do to trust anyone with your plans where the search for hidden gold was concerned. His uncle had found that out to his ultimate cost.

'Not long now, me fine bucko.' Mick's smile lit up his florid countenance as he eagerly scanned the horizon.

His buddy nodded. 'Won't come soon enough for me.'

The gleam in his eye was not lost on the Irishman whose curiosity had been aroused early on during the trek west.

Where was this young tenderfoot headed? And to what purpose? But Riley had kept his naturally inquisitive nature under wraps. Poking your snout into another man's trough was likely to get the said appendage pecked off.

The young jasper lit up another smoke, offering the sack of tobacco to Riley. The Irishman declined. Instead he extracted a blackened corncob from his pocket and proceeded to vigorously stoke it up.

A good ten years senior to his compadre, Mick Riley had come to America following the Great

Famine of 1846 that had decimated the Irish potato crop.

He had spent the years since struggling to survive in a city that took no prisoners. The gangs of New York had seen to that. Naturally he had gravitated to the Irish faction that went under the name of the Leprechauns, disparagingly labelled the Bogtrotters by rivals.

Riley had confided in his new sidekick that he had been forced to flee the city after stabbing one such adversary who never recovered. He had ended up in Leavenworth on the edge of the great wilderness. And like his friend, he was now working his way west to a new and, he hoped, better life.

A thick woollen shirt failed to conceal the Irishman's bulging torso. Muscles hard as iron had been tempered by the tough physical labour demanded from dock overseers along New York's busy waterfront.

They had met on the second day out from Leavenworth when Riley had come across the younger man being unmercifully harried. It was late afternoon. The wagons had camped up in a circle for the night and the young fellow had been taking a quiet stroll before supper when he had been accosted.

Such behaviour normally went with the territory where greenhorns were concerned. But when six burly teamsters, clearly the worse for drink, were observed resorting to unwarranted physical violence in pursuit of their fun, Riley felt obliged to step in.

'Leave him be!'

The brittle command brought the brutal intimidation to a sudden halt. Enunciated in a flat monotone. it sounded all the more chilling. The bullying teamsters turned to face the speaker.

It was the ringleader who spoke. His pockmarked visage was twisted into an ugly scowl made all the more sinister by a badly healed knife wound that gave his face a permanent sneer.

'Keep out of this, Riley.' he snarled, tapping a heavy club in the palm of his hand. 'Unless you want a taste of the same.' His associates ranged out in a half-circle behind their leader. The object of their derision was forgotten. 'There are six of us. You ain't got a chance if you wanna make some'n of it.'

Riley hunched down facing them. A large Bowie knife had suddenly appeared in his right hand. It wafted through the air, beams of sunlight glinting off the shiny steel blade.

'I'm figurin' that my friend here will even things up a little.' He prodded the razored point at the nearest man. 'So who's gonna be first to make his acquaintance?'

Relying on brute force alone to accomplish their hectoring of the young victim, the bullies took a step back. Six to one were mighty fine odds. But when the challenger was a hefty bogtrotting bruiser, the certainty of coming out of the fracas unscathed was substantially reduced.

At that moment the object of their scornful assault bounded upright. Grabbing hold of a dead tree branch, he swung it for all he was worth into the backs of the nearest of his assailants.

Thwack!

Three of them went down like ninepins. Out for the count and not likely to wake up in a hurry.

'That reduces the odds somewhat,' he announced, beaming brightly from ear to ear. Holding the weapon across his chest he quickly joined his Good Samaritan. 'Now who's next?'

The advantage had quickly switched sides. Bullies always need to have the edge. That had dissolved like sugar in a coffee mug. And the result was far less sweet to the palate. They backed off, uttering vague threats of future retribution whilst taking their downed comrades with them.

But Riley knew there would be no further attempts at intimidation. Respect had been earned.

'What was all that about?' he asked his new companion once they were alone.

'They didn't take kindly to an office worker having secured a muleskinner's job,' he replied. 'Thought I was too soft for manual work. Then there was my name.'

Riley gave him a puzzled frown.

The young greenhorn supplied him with the appendage.

'Horatio Muckleheimer.'

The Irishman's jaw dropped. Then he started to heehaw like a baying mule, slapping his thigh, unable to contain the bouts of gleeful laughter.

Muckleheimer stood there glowering. He was perplexed and bewildered, and looking none too pleased at this further ridicule of his name. Even at school he had been forced to defend the family honour in numerous playground battles. Not always the victor in such encounters, he had never once run away.

'What's so blamed funny?' he snapped waspishly. Fists clenched, he was all set to start another hoohah. 'I'm proud of who I am.'

The baying quickly subsided.

'It's sorry that I am for taking the piss, me young friend.' Riley raised his platelike hand in a conciliatory gesture. 'But you have to admit.' he added, shaking his head, 'with a name like that, is it any wonder the boys saw fit to taunt you? They just went too far, that's all.'

'Horatio Muckleheimer.' Riley repeated the name slowly, chewing on it like a piece of prime steak. 'Now ain't that a mouthful and no mistake.'

'My pa was a German immigrant,' asserted the younger man with evident pride. 'He had a huge respect for the English admiral following his defeat of the French at Trafalgar.'

'So Horatio it was.' Riley took a deep breath, his heavy brow furrowed in thought. 'Well, that has to change.'

'Huh?'

'We can't have you being accosted every time some turkey asks after your moniker. Not where you're bound. The Western frontier ain't no place for a fancy highfalutin handle like that.'

'So what do you suggest?' There was a hint of mordacity in the query.

'Nelson,' answered Riley, without any show of hesitation while boasting a cheesy grin wider than the Mississippi.

'Nelson what?'

'Just Nelson,' replied Riley, adding poignantly. 'Anyone calls you out, you've got the whole of the English nation to back you up.'

The young man wrapped his tongue around the famous nomenclature. He paused considering this novel change of circumstance, then nodded his agreement.

'Sounds good to me.'

They shook hands. So Horatio Muckleheimer was laid to rest, and resurrected as Nelson.

The two men stood side by side leaning on the back rail of the ferry. Riley's eagle eye followed that of his young comrade.

'I bet you these three silver dollars against that fine leather belt you's a-wearing,' Riley snorted, at the same time jingling the coins in his hand, 'that buzzard hawk catches hisself a lark within the next minute.' A huge grin split the florid complexion revealing creamy white gnashers. 'What d'yuh say then?' Again he rattled the coins.

Nelson parried the wry smirk with a weary sigh.

'Never give up, do you?' he said with a casual shake of the head. 'OK, it's a bet.' He spat on his hand and held it out. Riley seized it quickly to seal the wager.

Both men eyed the circling bird, just as they had done on numerous occasions throughout the trek. So far, Riley had lost every time. But he never gave up. An inveterate gambler.

And so it proved yet again.

Nelson held out his hand.

'You're never gonna get rich this way,' he chided, accepting his winnings. The Irishman offered a throwaway shrug of resignation.

'Easy come, easy go.'

At that precise moment the ferry bell pealed out to announce that they had reached the far side of the river.

'Time we were unloading,' announced Riley, setting his hat straight and buttoning his jacket. 'Can't be keeping the mules waiting.' He gave his young comrade a knowing wink. 'I heard tell we're due a bonus if the train reaches Santa Fe ahead of schedule. So we gotta keep our noses to the grindstone.' And with that breezy comment he disappeared to the far side of the ferry to check out the mules.

A wry smirk creased Nelson's face. He had come to regard the Irishman as a trusted friend. Maybe he ought to confide the real reason he was headed for Bronco Canyon. After all, he would need a sidekick to help him find the buried loot he was seeking. Cutting Mick Riley in for a piece of the action would be worth the help and back-up he could offer. Two months on the trail had brought the grim reality of his task firmly to the fore.

There was no way he could successfully pull it off alone.

TWO

CHEN SHING

Once the last of the wagons had been unloaded on to the west bank of the Pecos, the wagonmaster decided to make camp for the night. Soon a dozen cooking fires were ablaze. A rumbling stomach informed Nelson that it was getting close to chow time. Just as he was about to head off to locate his own mess crew, a scuffling accompanied by a muted cry at the far side of a clump of willow down by the river attracted his attention.

The pained yelp, no ordinary grunt of someone hard at work, was spiked with fear. Some poor sap was being manhandled. Nelson ducked behind a wagon as a tiny dwarf dashed into view. His small legs were no match for the group of well-dressed men that quickly caught and surrounded him.

Nelson recognized them as associates of Diamond Jim Garrison. The only son of the freight line owner, he had persuaded his father that his hell-raising days

16

were over. Caleb Garrison had been taken in by his son's apparent sincerity and put him in charge of the company's new venture along the Santa Fe Trail. But the old saying that a leopard never changes its spots was never truer than when applied to Jim Garrison.

Once the freighted goods had been sold in Santa Fe, Garrison intended keeping the profits for himself. His plan was to head West, setting himself up in business on the new gold field recently opened up near Mogollon in western New Mexico. Only his closest associates were privy to this clandestine skulduggery.

Ten years had passed since the initial discovery at Cushman Forge had transformed the territory. And now it was all about to begin afresh. Garrison intended to be there at the start. And not as a digger this time around. He had come to the conclusion that selling merchandise to those poor dupes was where the money was to be made.

Chen Shing was his personal servant. No higher than Nelson's waist, the diminutive Chinaman must have upset his boss for this fracas to have ensued.

'You thieving little bastard,' rasped Diamond Jim, aiming a hammer blow at the wriggling dwarf. The huge diamond stick-pin securing his neck tie glinted in the light pitched by the late sun. 'I'll teach you to steal from me.' Another backhander sent the little guy sprawling on to his back. 'Nobody takes my goods and gets away with it.'

Garrison was livid. His sidewhiskers bristled with unsuppressed anger.

'It not me, boss,' squealed Chen, raising his pudgy

17

arms in a futile effort to ward off the fearsome blows. Blood was pouring from a myriad cuts, his clothing was in tatters. '1 no take cheese from wagons.'

Garrison spat out a malicious laugh.

'Don't lie to me,' he railed. 'Three boxes are missing. And apart from me, you're the only other varmint who knows where they are stored.'

'Someone else must have taken them to get me in trouble,' yammered the Chinaman, frantically attempting to dodge the swinging clubs.

But Garrison was not listening.

He signalled to one of his confederates. A tall spindly dude handed him a coiled bullwhip. The men stood back forming a circle, their faces alight with bestial ardour. Garrison shook out the long brown serpent and flicked it. The ominous crack split the air.

'This is what happens to sticky-fingered skunks on my payroll.'

Nelson had heard enough.

Without thought for his own safety he emerged from his hiding place and leapt across the intervening few yards. Bundling aside the surrounding spectators to this grisly exhibition, he grabbed the whip from Garrison's hand.

'Nobody deserves this sort of treatment without a fair trial.' The young muleskinner's voice shook with nervous tension. 'Take him before the wagonmaster to answer any charge you have to make.' He peered around uncertainly, his nerve faltering. Nelson now realized that he had placed himself in a decidedly awkward situation.

But there was no going back.

The burly trader's face assumed the colour of a flaming sunset. He had been stunned into a mesmerized silence. Nobody challenged Diamond Jim Garrison. A growl akin to a grumbling volcano surged up from deep within his barrel chest, spewing forth an ugly torrent of choleric epithets.

More threatening as far as Nelson was concerned was the gun that appeared in his hand. Wide-eyed and staring, the young man wasted no further time in idle speculation as to the wisdom of his interference. He smashed the thickly knotted handle of the whip across the braggart's scowling mug.

Blood poured from the bully's smashed mouth. He slumped to the ground, arms flailing wildly.

Chen Shing had meanwhile scuttled out of the way and was eyeing the action fearfully from behind some bushes. All but forgotten in the mêlée that had ensued, he feared for his young benefactor's life whilst inwardly cursing himself for the coward that he was.

'I'll have the bastard!'

The stacatto yell came from Nelson's rear.

He swung to face the rush as an embittered ally of Garrison's came at him. But he was seconds too late. A blinding flash of agony pincered his brain as a lethal knife sliced through gristle and bone, tearing his innards to shreds. Nelson felt his legs going, his mind blanking off.

A voice seemed to echo in his brain from afar.

'Should I finish him off, boss?'

Garrison had recovered some of his composure as

he stumbled back on to his feet. A white silk hand-kerchief dabbed at his blooded face. The body-guard's knife hand was raised, ready to administer the *coup de grâce*.

'No need for that, Randy,' came back the firm resolve. 'Throw him in the river.' The trader uttered a manic guffaw. 'Let the bastard drown. It'll give him time to realize the folly of challenging Diamond Jim Garrison.'

Nelson was only vaguely aware of being dragged to the edge of the Pecos and flung headlong into the thrashing waters. It was this sudden cold dousing that jerked his lethargic brain back into gear. Panic lent urgency to his desparate situation. Stretching out an almost nerveless arm he managed somehow to fasten on to a drifting log before passing out again.

Drifting in and out of consciousness, Nelson knew that unless a miracle occurred he was a goner for sure.

It was pitch black. He was lying on what seemed like a sand bank, his lower body half covered by the clutching flow of the Pecos. At least he had plenty of water. No chance that he would die of thirst.

But what if the river level rose? The notion didn't bare thinking about.

And how long had he been here? One day or five, he had no way of knowing. Without food, his dwindling strength would quickly fade. Either that or he would bleed to death. He tried to move, but the effort propelled waves of agony through his mangled entrails. Time passed in a dazed stupor. And with each passing hour he was growing ever weaker.

Then.

Just when all hope seemed lost, an alien sound penetrated his stupefied brain. Was it a scavenging coyote scuffling in the darkness, sensing a tasty meal in the offing? Or maybe his mind playing macabre tricks?

Heavy breathing informed him that it was a human presence. Somebody raised his head and wiped a damp cloth over his fevered brow.

Then a match flared. The injured man shrank back from the harsh light. 'It is good that you are still alive.'

It was the high-pitched lilting cadence of the little Chinaman. Nelson opened his eyes half-expecting to discover it was all an illusion, that he had passed over into some kind of netherworld.

But this was no figment of his tortured brain. The beaming eyes, the jaundiced colouring of the skin, the wide mouth, lips tight with suppressed anxiety, told a different tale.

'How long have I been here?' croaked Nelson. His voice sounded distant, an extraneous rumble.

'Three days. I could not come sooner.' He lifted Nelson's shoulders and wiped away the congealed blood with a damp cloth before hurrying on. 'Garrison has found the cheese. It was wrongly stored which gets me, how you say. . . .' His large plate-like head bobbed in thought

'. . . off the hook?' suggested Nelson trying to summon up a smile.

'Yes, yes. That is it. Off the darned hook,' shot

back the little guy. 'But he no apologize. Just kick me more saying it my fault.'

The strange little fellow bristled angrily. His jaws snapped with fiery indignation. Then he quickly extracted some disinfectant and bandaging from the folds of his black smock. Deftly and with care, he proceeded to clean and dress the knife wound.

It was clear that the muleskinner had lost a lot of blood. But he was young. And having been delivered from the jaws of death, he was damned if the grim reaper was going to mark his card now.

'What is your name?' asked Nelson chewing on a lump of the 'stolen' cheese.

'Chen Shing,' replied the dwarf, tying off a bandage. 'It mean Great Victory.'

Nelson smiled knowingly. It figured. This little dude was one tough cookie. And he proceeded to display his innate vigor by assisting his patient to his feet. In a series of shorts bursts, Chen Shing half-carried, half-dragged Nelson away from the river's edge. The unlikely duo eventually found themselves in a small cave, no more than two yards deep, but sufficient to keep them dry. A crescent moon peeped invitingly through a break in the clouds.

'Where are we?' enquired Nelson peering around.

'About five miles south of Conchas.' Chen Shing helped Nelson out of his wet clothes and under a blanket. Then he gathered kindling for a fire. 'Nobody likely to come after you now. Garrison assume you drowned, and figured Chen Shing deserted. That true!' he asserted vehemently. 'And at earliest opportunity. Then come to find brave muleskinner who saved miserable bacon.'

Nelson attempted a laugh, the effort eliciting a pained groan.

After comfortably settling his patient the little man made to fix supper. It was some time later, after they had eaten, that Nelson was able to reflect on the circumstances that had brought him here.

'How can I thank you enough?' he muttered, tears welling in his eyes. 'You saved my life.'

Chen Shing shrugged his wide shoulders. 'One debt repay another. Chinese proverb say, rich is man who repays a kindness. Poor man look other way.'

Then he left to feed the pair of mules he had stolen from the wagon train. They would be needed to reach Santa Fe.

During the next seven days Nelson stayed within the confines of the cave under the somewhat unorthodox care of the little Chinaman. Occasional riders could be seen on the east bank of the Pecos. But luckily no unwelcome vistors ever came near the cave.

On the eighth day, Nelson announced that he felt fit enough to travel. By taking things at a slow pace, they should reach Santa Fe in a week.

Chen Shing explained that the disappearance of the muleskinner had been easily explained away by Diamond Jim. He had instructed his confederates to spread the word that the teamster had been seen on the banks of the Pecos and must have fallen in after a drinking session. It being his birthday and all.

The Chinaman had been in two minds whether to tell Mick Riley the truth. But the astute dwarf had decided to hold his peace. Tongues wag on a wagon train, and the tenacious Irishman might have had difficulty containing his unpredictable temper. Nelson agreed that he had done the right thing.

THREE

GATEWAY TO EL DORADO

When the legendary town of Santa Fe eventually hove into view, Nelson became edgier than a Mexican jumping bean. He had no way of knowing whether Garrison was still there. They waited on a bluff above the town until nightfall. Only after the sun had set did they mount up and cajole the recalcitrant mules back into motion.

'D'you figure Garrison will still be around?' Nelson enquired nervously.

'You not worry,' soothed the dwarf to allay his fears. 'He got firm orders from father to return to Leavenworth soon as goods sold.'

'If I ever come across that skunk again,' snarled Nelson, 'he'll rue the day he crossed swords with Horatio Muckleheimer.'

'Come,' urged Chen, leading the way down

towards the scattered lights of Santa Fe. 'Time not ripe for thoughts of vengeance.'

A full moon had nudged the clouds aside, bathing the town in a silvery glow. From afar, the distant hum of a bustling frontier town in full flow heralded their arrival. Lights twinkled along the main street as they approached the outer limits of the town, a mesmeric invitation after months on the trail.

Nelson breathed deeply. He had arrived at last in the real West that he had always dreamed about.

Cautiously, they nudged the mules forward, keeping to the edge of the wide main street.

Their first task was to find a suitable place to stay.

This posed no problems. Santa Fe was a cosmopolitan settlement, used to the comings and goings of all manner of nationalities and its Chinese sector was well established.

It was to this part of the town that Chen Shing headed. He was confident that his outlandish appearance would receive no adverse comment from his own race. Indeed the little man was positively welcomed by the proprietor of the first place to which he called. It was a back-street hotel boasting the tantalizing name of the Lotus Flower.

Once established. Nelson announced that he was keen to locate his old buddy, even though it was well into the early hours.

'Where do you figure that big galoot will have headed once he got paid off?' enquired Nelson, rubbing his hands in avid anticipation.

'Like all muleskinners.' responded the dwarf with a wry smirk, 'He will head for the nearest saloon.'

Nelson jumped to his feet. 'Let's go then!' He likewise was ready for a few drinks and a solid meal.

Chen Shing held up a cautionary hand.

'Prudent is the man who looks before he leaps.'

The tenderfoot gave a sigh of exasperation.

'Do you Orientals always have to talk in riddles?'

'We are both tired, my impetuous friend, and need a good night's rest.' The little man then pointed to Nelson's blood-smeared and ragged apparel. 'And you in bad need of decent clothes.'

Nelson angled a critical eye at his dissolute appearance. Following a disconcerting examination, he gave an abashed nod.

'OK! OK!' he averred. 'So you're right as usual.'

He lay down on one of the single beds, suddenly overcome with fatigue. A combination of stress, exhaustion and the severe injury had suddenly come home to roost. His eyes closed. In less time than it takes to say gold nuggets, he was fast asleep.

Next morning Nelson awoke to the yammer of a cats' chorus outside his window. He rubbed the grit from his eyes.

Chen Shing had risen early. He had already been out and picked up a set of duds from a used clothing warehouse. As expected, they fitted perfectly. Nelson dipped his head into a basin of water. A thorough dousing removed the cobwebs from his torpid brain.

His first port of call was the nearest café, and a proper breakfast. No more of that awful slop served up on the trail. The place that had attracted his attention lay across the street from their lodgings. It boasted a garishly painted sign announcing the *finest vittles west of everywhere* with Lizzy Jo Clayborne as sole proprietor.

The café was busy but they managed to secure a table by the window.

'You fellas new in town?' The hearty greeting originated from a large, blousy woman of indeterminate age. Well-rounded in every sense, this was obviously the celebrated Lizzy Jo. And she clearly enjoyed her own cooking.

'Just got in last night,' replied Nelson.

'Where you from?'

'Leavenworth. We're with the Sovereign Freight Line.'

'You a muleskinner, then?'

'Could be,' iterated Nelson, less than happy with the cross-examination he was receiving.

Lizzy Jo towered over the customers, hands resting on her amply padded hips. Eyebrows caked in black lifted like a pair of raven wings.

'Sovereign, yer say?' The reply was more a statement of fact than a question. 'We had a guy in here last night from that crew,' she added with a troubled shake of the head. Blond curls floated in the hot atmosphere like a ripening field of corn.

This time it was Nelson's turn to offer a surprised look.

'What his name?' cut it Chen Shing.

'Didn't ask,' replied Lizzy. 'But he was Irish and already half-cut when he tumbled in here. Asked after the makings of an all-night poker school.'

'Riley!' came back the immediate dual response.

'You acquainted with this guy?'

'Sure are,' replied Nelson.

'I pointed him in the direction of the Black Dog saloon on West Portland Street. They run an honest game.' Her booming cadence lowered abruptly to a warning hiss. 'Unlike a heap of other dung pits in this town I could mention.' The cook wagged a pudgy finger at her guests. 'If'n this guy is a friend of your'n, you'd be well advised to watch out for him. To my practised eye, he's got loser stamped right across the middle of his forehead.'

'Don't I know it,' muttered Nelson.

After shovelling down a king-sized portion of prime rib smothered in fried potatoes and washed down by a gallon of strong coffee, he was ready for a Havana cigar to finish it off.

'Boy, that sure hit the mark.' he said with a contented sigh.

A raucous belch indicated his unqualified approval of the bounteous feast to all and sundry.

Lizzy Jo's over-rouged mush split into a beaming grin.

'Glad you enjoyed it, fella,' she responded, handing over a business card. 'Be obliged if'n you'd spread the word.'

'One more thing,' asked Nelson in a more cautious tone of voice.

'Yeah?'

'Do you happen to have seen a big snappily dressed dude sporting a diamond stick pin in town?'

There was no hesitation in Lizzy Jo's curt response.

'Jim Garrison!' The name emerged more like a choking growl. 'Now there's one mean-assed son of

Satan. You guys would be well advised to keep away from that slime ball. He's poison and no mistake.'

'Is he still in town?'

'Far as I know he left two days ago,' she said. 'Put it around that he was heading back to Leavenworth now his business in Santa Fe was finished.'

Nelson gave a satisfied nod. Chen had been right.

After paying for the repast, the two amigos left the eating house. Nelson's ruddy cheeks glowed with a sublime expression as he peered up and down Santa Fe's renowned Española Street. The place was packed to the gills with all manner of jiggers, the vast majority just passing through. Santa Fe was a jumping-off point for those heading west to the goldfields.

Nelson stood for a moment imbibing the heady atmosphere.

For every mercantile emporium, there was a saloon with such colourful appendages as the Golden Sunset, the Whale Tail and the Devil's Kitchen. Only at the far end of the street could be found the premises catering to the needs of the freighting companies.

One thought that immediately struck the young man was that everybody was sporting a firearm of some sort. Riley had warned him of the need to be thus similarly accoutred, not to mention his Uncle Jeb. Even though he had never owned one before, he now felt exposed, only half-dressed.

Luckily, next door to the café was a gun shop. And, in the window, all manner of pistols, large and small.

With his few remaining dollars Nelson invested in a second-hand .36 calibre Navy Colt, including a supply of firing caps and ready-made lead balls. The gunsmith took him out back and gave him some rudimentary instruction in the use of the revolver and its loading. A wary shake of the head followed the smiling young greenhorn back on to the street. The shopkeeper clearly did not have much faith that his lesson would be successfully followed through.

Nelson proudly eyed his new purchase.

Chen Shing was less enthusiastic. His mottled features creased into a bleak frown. The Chinaman's disquiet was lost on Nelson who stuck the gun into its holster and strutted off down the covered boardwalk. He was now one of the crowd.

'Let's go find Riley,' crowed the young man, setting his battered Stetson at a jaunty angle.

Chen Shing waggled after him, his short bow legs doing nineteen to the dozen. He received a few sniggers and pointed fingers but nobody physically accosted him. The shiny Colt slung around his comrade's waist was sufficient to dissuade all but the stupid or dead drunk. Had they known that Nelson had never in his life fired a gun in anger, things might have been different. At that moment in time, the young tenderfoot had blind self-assurance and naïvité as to the ways of the frontier on his side.

Thus far they were proving to be questionable allies.

A short amble to the north found them at a junction.

Chen Shing pointed up at the street sign.

'West Portland.' Nelson nodded, turning inland away from the noise of the main drag. 'The Black

31

Dog must be up here someplace.'

The gambling den was two blocks along on the far side. And they were none too soon in arriving.

'Ain't that . . .' Nelson jabbed a finger at a tousle-headed inebriate pursuing a somewhat erratic course along the middle of the narrow street. Bespattered with mud, the guy was completely oblivious to his surroundings. His attempted rendition of a famous Irish ditty bore little resemblance to the original.

'Mick Riley!' Chen Shing had also recognized the lurching form. 'He in bad shape.'

Nelson was about to call his friend when the dwarf stayed his outburst with a quick jerk on his coat sleeve.

Nelson eyed him quizzically. Then he followed the direction of the little man's prodding finger.

Three men were furtively shadowing the weaving drunk. Tough hardcases, their intentions towards the Irishman were clearly not of the benevolent variety. It was obvious that they had followed Riley out of the saloon and were intent on bushwhacking him. Maybe, for once, he had managed to discover the elusive luck of the Irish.

That piece of good fortune was about to be violently terminated. Unless Nelson and his partner intervened. But what could they do?

Blood drained from the young tenderfoot's visage, leaving him ashen-faced and tense. Here was being played out the true nature of the frontier in all its brutal reality.

Nelson drew to a halt. He was stunned into immobility. The three assailants had stepped down into the muddy street. Even though they each sported a holstered pistol, heavy wooden clubs were their preferred weapons. A silent attack would enable them to escape unobserved.

Or so they had thought.

It was Chen Shing who offered a solution to their dilemma.

'I will draw off the fat one with some choice remark concerning his eating habits. Coming from Chinaman, that direst of insults.' He rattled off the rest of his plan quickly, short arms frantically wind-milling. 'You must challenge other two. Stop them any way you can with that new shooter.' He jerked Nelson back to the actuality of their situation. 'Can do? Can do?' he hissed frantically.

'S-sure, sure,' stuttered Nelson, shrugging off the lethargy that had threatened to overwhelm his taut muscles. 'You go ahead. Don't worry none. I'll get the drop on the other two.'

Jumping down into the street, Chen Shing hollered at the three bruisers. 'Hey fat boy!'

His strident tones cut through the early morning heat haze.

The larger of the river rats immediately swung on his heel. He knew instantly that the affront was meant for him. It had happened before. And there were plenty of sore heads that would not be repeat-ing that mistake. His ugly mug glowered angrily at the speaker.

'You talkin' to me, Chink?' he snarled.

'Who else in street look like tub of lard?' The little fellow followed up his mordacious effrontery with an

33

obscene gesture. 'Fat spoofer has stuffed down too many cow pies, fit to burst any time now.' A raucous cackle broke free as Chen sidled purposefully towards a gap between two buildings.

The thug's bulging torso shook, his livid features contorting with rage. The robbery was forgotten. Nobody spoke to Crusher McGee like that, least of all a slimy Chink. And a dwarf to boot.

A manic growl bubbled from Crusher's throat. He almost choked on his own wrath. Swinging the wicked bludgeon in preparation for living up to his eminently suited nickname, he made to cross the street. His only thought, to wipe the oily smirk from the little runt's warped visage.

Another insulting gesture from Chen Shing was the last straw for Crusher McGee. Purple veins throbbed in his bullish neck as the ungainly hulk rumbled across the street. But he was whistling in the wind.

With one last wave the Chinaman disappeared, knowing that his pursuer was unable to follow. The gap between the buildings was far too constricted for all but the smallest individual to squeeze through. The little man had picked up on this right away. Being on the diminutive side had its advantages.

The other two hardcases had likewise been taken by surprise at this unforeseen frustration of their nefarious scheme. They stood open-mouthed as the little man jumped about like a dancing flea as he castigated their porcine confederate.

Nelson sucked in a couple of deep breaths, girded himself, then let fly his own harsh invective. Just like he'd read in numerous lurid novelettes, the baddies always caved in to a hard, brittle command.

'Drop those staves and shuck your hardware,' he rapped, injecting a taut stacatto rush into his delivery. He fully expected the varmints to cower back and instantly obey.

But this was not the land of make-believe.

Both of the bushwhackers spun to face this new threat. One discarded his club whilst drawing and firing his pistol. The other was more aware of the potential danger. He backed off a pace but tripped over a cat. The startled animal emitted a fearful screech, then fled the scene.

Two bullets discharged from the first thug's pistol gouged large chunks of wood from the veranda upright that was partly concealing the young greenhorn. Nelson froze. This wasn't supposed to happen. A third shot singed his left arm. The searing pain of hot lead was enough to kickstart a response.

Eyes closed, he gripped the revolver with both hands and aimed it in the general direction of his adversaries.

Aim, cock and fire! Aim, cock and fire!

Just like the gunsmith said.

Six times the Colt bucked in his hands. Black powder smoke filled the street as the six loud reports bounced off the enclosing wooden façades. Only when the hammer clicked on to an empty cylinder did Nelson deign at last to cease firing.

A tight silence filled the air.

When the haze lifted the would-be thief was splayed out in the muddy street face down. It was obvious, even to a greenhorn like Nelson, that he was dead. The gun slipped from nerveless fingers as the full import of what he had done penetrated his numbed brain.

Upon witnessing the brusque dispatch of his confederate, the third sewer rat made a rapid exit up a nearby alley.

'Look out! Behind you!'

The slurred warning came from Mick Riley. Gunfire and raised voices had cleared his addled head enough to assimilate the dangerous situation he had caused.

Nelson's brain had shut down. His mind was in a fog. The warning passed unheard. But not by Chen Shing. The little man had re-emerged from the constricted passage to witness Crusher McGee palming a heavy Walker Colt. The massive gun lifted effortlessly. And at that range, the big thug couldn't miss the static target of Horatio Muckleheimer.

The dwarf wasted no time. In a single deadly movement a thin stilleto was spinning through the air to bury itself in the hardcase's broad back. The gun erupted. But its aim was spoilt as the big jasper tottered, then collapsed in a heap. The bullet drilled a hole in Nelson's boot heel, jerking him back to reality.

Downtown Santa Fe was no stranger to gunfire. But such events always drew a crowd of sightseers, all agog to witness the spilling of blood. Just so long as it wasn't their own.

'Did you see that?' called one excited dude at the back.

'Fanciest shootin' I ever did see,' extolled another pushing forward eagerly to slap the young shootist on the back.

'And he even did it with his eyes fast shut,' agreed a third.

In the excitement, Chen Shing's part in the fracas was ignored. His despised nationality, not to mention diminutive size, assured the Chinaman of the anonymity he nonetheless welcomed.

The crowd swelled as word of the young gunfighter's prowess rapidly spread down the street. The two friends were eagerly hustled into the Black Dog to celebrate. With free drinks on offer, neither bothered to enlighten the crowd regarding the true nature of the encounter. For the moment, the two deceased bushwhackers were forgotten. Just another pair of hard-nosed vipers whose luck had run dry.

FOUR

A DEAL IS STRUCK

It was some two hours later, following their return to the lodging house in Chinatown when Riley explained why he had become a potential ambush victim. He extracted a large Havana cigar from his inside pocket, inhaled the aroma, then lit up.

'I heard there was an all-night poker game running at the Black Dog,' he began sipping a mug of strong black coffee.

'So we discovered,' interjected Nelson, rolling his eyes.

'And who be telling you that then?' retorted the mystified Irishman. He shook the torpor from his fuzzy head. The coffee was beginning to produce the desired effect.

It was Chen Shing who elaborated in his usual eloquent manner. 'Chinese proverb say: if want to keep secret safe, tell not to woman.'

'What woman?' questioned Riley, screwing his face

into a perplexed grimace.

'We ate at the same café as you,' explained Nelson.

'Ah yes.' Riley nodded affecting the wisdom of hindsight. 'Lizzy Jo Clayborne. A fine figure of a woman and no mistake. And a good cook.'

'But woman all same,' warned the Chinaman sagely. 'Although on this occasion, proverb thankfully confused.'

'So about this poker game.' Nelson was keen to discover what had occurred in the Black Dog. 'Did you find it?'

Riley nodded. He puffed on the large cigar. The wraith of blue smoke mingled delicately with the floating dust motes.

'See-sawed all night through,' he iterated with eager enthusiasm. 'One minute I was losing, the next winning. Then, around dawn, I hit the jackpot. Lady luck was a-sitting right there on my shoulder. Couldn't do nothing wrong. Boy oh boy! Were them cards singing.'

Riley suddenly broke off. He sat back in his chair, a numinous expression tempering the squinting features.

Nelson and the dwarf were left on tenterhooks.

'Well?' exclaimed Nelson, unable to contain his impatience. 'So what happened?'

'Won me a packet, didn't I?' Then in a sombre tone. 'Them skunks must have been watching out just so's they could bust a jackass like me.'

Silence followed as the three buddies digested the import of their recent encounter. Even though the demise of the sewer rats would be judged a case of self-defence in law, Chen Shing was all for leaving town at the earliest opportunity. No sense in tempting fate.

'Where you headed then?'

This from Nelson, who had likewise been giving the matter a great deal of consideration. Although a hell's-a-poppin' burg like Santa Fe was well used to such happenings, killing was frowned upon by the powers that be. Like as not, they would be encouraged to leave anyway.

'I heard there has been a new gold strike up at Mogollon,' replied the little guy. 'Good chance to set up Chinese eating house.'

Riley chuckled to himself. 'Mind if I join up with you, Chop Suey?' He laid emphasis on the nickname whilst giving the dwarf a wry smirk.

Chen Shing's whole body tensed. A chilly atmosphere suddenly came over the room. For a brief moment the Chinaman's warped features assumed a grim cast, the slanted eyes narrowing to black slits. Like Nelson, he was proud of his oriental heritage. And took umbrage at any disparagement.

Then, just as quickly, he relaxed as a beaming smile spread across the annular façade.

'Nickname mean I one of the boys?' he enquired clapping his little hands in glee.

'Sure does,' replied Riley breezily.

'That good. We now all friends together.'

'Figure I might get in on the diggings before all the best claims are staked,' proferred Riley after due consideration. 'Reckon the winnings from the Black Dog will buy me a grubstake. What about you, Nelson?'

This was the moment to which the young mule-skinner had been building. He looked at the two men sitting opposite. His keen gaze was both penetrating and reflective. Each of them was completely different in character from the other. Yet each had proved to be worthy of the highest trust. And it was abundantly clear that he would need help if his uncle's legacy was to be forthcoming.

He took a deep breath. Then he launched headlong into the bizarre tale revealed in Jeb Stockwell's mysterious communication.

At the end of the narrative, he produced the all-important epistle as proof that this was no chimera.

'You read it out, Chop Suey,' said Riley handing the envelope to his new partner. 'I ain't so good with the words.'

The dwarf carefully read out the contents, then studied the enclosed map. 'This Bronco Canyon on the Natanes Plateau over border in Arizona,' he said. There was a hint of reservation in the statement.

Riley's thick lips puckered. 'Man, that's one bad place.' He shook his head. 'Too hot even for Old Nick himself. Go in there, Nelson, me fine feller, and the odds are you won't be comin' out.'

'So what if all three of us go,' broached the young man, slowly emphasizing each word. 'An even partnership split three ways. This is no wild-goose chase. The gold is there, just awaiting for someone to uncover it. Ain't that worth the risk?'

Riley's jaw dropped.

'You want me and Chop Suey here to join up with you and go after this here treasure trove? Is that what you're sayin'?'

Nelson held out his hand.

'What do you say then?' he asked eyeing them both hopefully. 'Is it a deal?'

Riley eyeballed the dwarf whose mouth had like-wise flapped open. Then he grabbed a bottle of whiskey and poured himself a generous measure and downed the fiery tipple in a single throw.

'You got yourself a partner, boy.' Riley's enthusi-asm was salient.

'Two partners better still,' added Chen Shing.

'Yeehaar!' howled Nelson lustily. 'We're on our way. All for one and one for all.'

A triple handshake was the clincher with Riley agreeing to bankroll the expedition for an extra cut of the proceeds.

Two days later they were heading out of town on the stagecoach. Only recently had it begun operating, since news of the gold strike had filtered back from Mogollon. Because of the rough nature of the terrain in the foothills of the Tularosa Range, it only went as far as Quemado. From there, prospectors would have to find an alternative means of transport.

Three other gold-hungry prospectors were also on the stage. All talk was of the strike and the riches that were within their grasp.

For one old-timer, this was his third expediton. The other pair were taking on their first attempt at gold prospecting. In consequence the old jasper commanded their unwavering attention. And he took full advantage of the captive audience to expand on his knowledge and experience, waxing lyrical about the huge nuggets just sitting on the creek beds waiting to be picked up.

When asked why he was heading back to the gold fields, rheumy eyes had misted over as he recalled the loss of not one but two fortunes.

'Easy come easy go, boys!' was the casual comment, accompanied by a nonchalent shrug. 'It's the thrill of the search that's half the pleasure.' He sighed as past memories were recalled. 'Keeps drawing me back every time I hears of a new strike. Like as not it'll be the same until they buries me in a pine box. There goes Sourdough Lannigan. And on my tombstone they can carve the epitaph: He Never Gave Up!'

Sourdough accepted the cigar offered by Mick Riley.

'You fellers aimin' to try your luck as well?' he enquired of the three partners who had been equally enthralled by the old guy's breezy repartee.

'Not us,' replied the Irishman with solid conviction. 'We're after—'

A surreptitious dig in the ribs from his diminutive *compadre* brought the utterance to an abrupt halt.

'What my friend mean is that we start up restaurant in Mogollon,' Chen Shing hurried on as the Irishman realized that his enthusiasm had run away with him, almost stymying their plans. The last thing they wanted was to instigate another gold rush into Bronco Canyon. A loose tongue was what had started the initial flurry of activity at Cashman Forge ten years earlier.

The old prospector appeared not to have noticed anything untoward. He was a mine of information for the greenhorn gold-seekers, and more than happy to regale them with a host of colourful stories. Frequent pulls from a hip flask ensured that they became ever more lurid and sensational as time passed.

Along the trail they passed innumerable other prospectors, all heading in the same direction. Some were leading heavily laden packmules. Most were on foot, toting worldly possessions on their backs. Not since the big rush of '49 had gold fever been this strong.

Most of the camps that had sprung up along the foothills of the Tularosa Mountains had died off as the gold had become exhausted. The stagecoach passed through a host of ghost towns, their weathered buildings deserted and rotting in the harsh New Mexico sun.

Mogollon was one of the few towns that had received a much needed boost following the recent discovery. But it was off the beaten trail and it would involve a further five days of hard trekking across the lower foothill country for the travellers to complete the journey.

After three days of rough travel the stagecoach eventually entered the disparate collection of hutments known as Quemado. The single main street was flanked by a warren of interconnected alleys and ginnels. None of the buildings were constructed of brick, giving the town an air of impermanence. Street lighting was non-existent. And many of the deep ruts extending the full length of the main drag were full of water following a recent flash storm.

All this was of little consequence to the new arrivals. The first step of their trip to gloryland had been accomplished.

Excitement gripped the passengers, even Sourdough Lannigan. As the coach drew to a halt outside the stage depot the doors were flung open.

'OK, folks,' announced the driver. 'This is Quemado, end of the line. Anybody headin' up to the new strike in Mogollon will have to hire mules. Or hoof it. I'll be back next month for those who have come to your senses.'

'Agh!' spat the old prospector. 'Don't you fellers be takin' any notice of that critter. He's only jealous 'cos he ain't got neither the guts nor the stamina of a true miner.'

Tossing his haversack over a stooped shoulder, the old guy trundled off in search of the nearest saloon. He was dogged by the two greenhorns whom he had promised to assist with their provisioning.

For Nelson the trip from Santa Fe had been an ever-worsening nightmare. The knife wound he had sustained courtesy of Diamond Jim Garrison had reopened and was bleeding badly. And fever had set in with a vengeance. His position was not helped by the hard wooden seats in a means of transport that had been little more than a covered wagon.

Rest and the ministrations of a sawbones were desperately needed. There was no way that the three partners could continue their journey until Nelson was fully recovered. Riley procured the services of the only doctor in town who informed him that recuperation would take at least a month.

Until then, they would be forced to kick their heels in Quemado.

FIVE

BAD LUCK FOR BODIE

Chen Shing managed to secure employment helping the cook at a local diner. Being Chinese he was able to offer a variation to the menu that was much appreciated by the owner. Such was the increase in custom that he was offered a permanent position.

The little guy was sorely tempted.

While he was assiduously adding to the coffers of the three gold-seekers, Riley had succumbed to his old ways. By the time that Nelson was sufficiently well to continue their journey, he had frittered away most of his previous winnings.

Chen Shing was incensed. The three of them were sitting in the dwarf's room nursing a bottle of cheap hooch.

'You foolish Irishman,' he railed, leaping into the air like a demented puppet. It would have been a funny sight but for the seriousness of the situation. 'Why you waste grubstake like that while I work butt off in diner? All my money go to pay doctor's bill and hotel rooms. And all you can do is hand over to gambling man in saloon.'

Riley ignored the jibe, his face displaying a blank expresson of bewilderment.

'I can't figure it out,' he said, offering a limp shrug of the shoulders. 'On a heap of occasions I was darned certain I had the makings of a winning hand. And every time, that pesky gambler came up with a better one.' He scratched his head. 'I was watching him like a hawk. If'n the rat was cheating I never saw how he did it.'

The Chinaman quickly simmered down. Sipping the hard liquor and relishing its sharp bite, he stroked his jutting chin in thought.

'Maybe lost winnings not all your fault.' Chen Shing had much experience of shady dealings after serving under Diamond Jim Garrison. And he was inclined to believe the Irishman's vigorous protestations that some kind of chicanery was afoot. 'How much you got left?' he asked eventually.

Riley's bluff features reddened, his large feet shuffling nervously. His response to Chen Shing's query was hesitant. Silently he turned out his pockets. Empty as a church on payday.

Nelson could barely contain a wry smile.

The dwarf sighed. Then he dug into his own pocket and offered Riley a handful of dollar bills.

'Go play another game,' he said. 'And this time, we turn tables on cheating cardsharp.'

'How you figuring to do that?'

'You just play game, let Chop Suey do thinking.'

'Don't forget me,' butted in Nelson, checking the load on his pistol. 'I'll keep an eye on things from a distance.'

His two partners eyed each other with blunt scepticism.

'Just watch where you're pointing that thing,' muttered Riley.

Nelson shrugged off the implied challenge to his shooting prowess. After all, hadn't he seen off that gang in Santa Fe?

The next hour was spent huddled over a pot of strong coffee as they discussed the way forward.

Three horses were to be purchased from the livery stable by Nelson. Both associates had managed to persuade him that keeping watch outside the saloon with the mounts ready for a quick exit was a far more vital role under the circumstances.

It was well known that many of the new gold settlements were subject to vigilante law. But there was no way of predicting the outcome of such bar room court proceedings. They might well be labelled as troublemakers and made to pay the consequences. Better to quit the scene as soon as possible, and with a full pocket.

During the thrashing out of their plan to thwart the slippery gambler, Riley made surreptitious attempts to liven up the brew with a belt of whiskey. His efforts were met with vehement hostility from the Chinaman.

'You need all wits for showdown if we to escape

with skin in one piece,' he expostulated firmly. 'You forgot about Black Dog already?'

Riley's face crinkled at the recollection.

As if on cue to confirm the serious nature of their plans, lightning crackled overhead. It was followed soon after by the ominous rumble of thunder. New Mexico was well known for its arid climate, but flash floods were a not uncommon occurrence in the foothills of the mountains.

Many camps erected on the banks of such outflows had been washed away. But this was how much of the yellow temptation was laid down. And as such it was all the easier to extract by hordes of fortune seekers who flooded into the diggings.

The first heavy drops rattled against the window.

'You still in this game, feller?'

A natty dude sporting a black goatee beard with matching heavy eyebrows had addressed the thoughtful Irishman sitting opposite. His name was Black Jack Bodie on account of that being his favourite game. Two other players made up the game. Having thrown in their hands, each of them was keenly studying the other two.

The pot had risen to $500. No mean sum in a small burg like Quemado. Riley glanced up from his cards and studied the smirking coyote opposite. Black Jack was giving nothing away. Only the constant twitching of his left eye intimated that the pressure of the game was beginning to tell. An irritating distraction for Riley who was earnestly trying to work out how the bastard worked his scam.

Smoke drifted in the fetid air of the room. Brown tendrils swirled in the lamplight under the low ceiling. All around the noisy hubbub of a saloon in full swing continued, totally unaffected by the tension at the gaming table.

'Well, pilgrim?' asked the gambler, injecting a hint of impatience into the query. 'What's it to be? You gotten the bottle, or are you just time-wasting? We ain't got all day.'

His aim was to faze his opponent, unsettle him. The ruse was working. But not on account of the gambler's churlishness.

When was Chop Suey going to play his own inimitable hand in the proceedings? The game had been under way for over an hour and the Irishman's pot was almost empty.

Chen Shing's plan had been to give Riley ample opportunity to fully immerse himself in the game. Money had changed hands, with all concerned winning some and losing some. That was the gambler's ploy. Make himself appear clean as a new pin. Then he would move in for the final clean-up.

And that time had arrived.

Chen Shing's hawkish gaze recognized the signs. The tightness around the jawline, the narrowing eyes like cold chips of black ice. Gingerly he slipped beneath the batwing doors bending low as he scuttled silently around close to the wooden walls. He seemed no more than an opaque blur, merging into the dun background – yet another advantage of his diminutive stature. Nobody noticed the shadowy figure as it slid beneath the gaming table.

The eyes of all the players were fixed, unmoving, on the cards. Chen Shing waited. His whole body was tensed up like a coiled spring. Carefully he removed the long narrow stiletto from his belt.

Then it happened.

The gambler's left hand slid beneath the table and palmed a pair of kings from a secret pocket in his trousers. Just as casually, they were replaced by a three of hearts and a seven of spades.

From a distance the little man could hear the gambler urging his opponent to make his play. This was his moment.

Without hesitation, he plunged the dagger into the outstretched palm that was still clutching the two illicit discards. The blade penetrated the hand. And such was the force of the thrust that it jabbed straight through and into the gambler's leg.

A scream of pain was wrenched from the injured man's open mouth. Blood spurted from the wounds.

But the slimy toad was not finished yet. Ever the consummate professional, Black Jack shrugged off the violent shock of the assault. With his free hand he reached into a pocket and extracted a stubby single-shot pistol. Of only .32 calibre, it nonetheless could be lethal at short range. Pushing back his chair, the cardsharp pointed the gun at Riley.

But his reactions had been slowed. The jolt to his system from the knife thrust was rapidly taking effect. It gave Riley sufficient time to draw his own revolver and loose off a couple of shots. The double blast rocked the saloon. Bodie lurched backwards toppling across a roulette table.

The Irishman had the foresight to shoot out the coal-oil lantern that was the sole source of illumination at the rear of the saloon.

A chaotic mêlée of shouting and jostling immediately ensued. Nobody was quite sure what had occurred. Taking advantage of the darkness, Chen Shing grabbed up the pile of banknotes on the table, then disappeared.

'Who's doing all that shooting?' howled the bartender.

'Has someone been killed?' enquired a gruff voice to Riley's left.

Gunsmoke mingling with that from innumerable cigarillos served to create an opaque, almost surreal atmosphere that enabled the instigators of the uproar to slip away unseen.

A light flared as someone struck a match.

'Its the house gambler!' exclaimed a loud voice. 'He's bin shot and stabbed.' It was not long before the true nature of the violent confrontation emerged.

By that time Riley and his tiny comrade were outside. Nelson bundled the little guy into the saddle, then mounted up himself. Riley was already frantically spurring his own cayuse down the main street.

That was the moment the heavens chose to open their gates. Heavy droplets of rain bouncing off the hard-packed dirt street quickly gathered momentum. The deluge that followed was to prove a blessing in disguise. In no time, they were soaked to the skin. But in such a cascading downpour, there was little chance of them being pursued, assuming that any witnesses knew the direction they had taken.

For the next half-hour they kept up a blistering pace. Heading in a general westerly direction, they urged their mounts to maintain a steady gallop. Only when they were well clear of the town did Riley lead them off the trail into a narrow draw thick with pine and juniper trees.

Within the confines of a secluded grove they were able to find shelter. A fire was soon blazing, steam rising from wet clothes as the three partners huddled together gratefully absorbing the welcome heat.

Chop Suey lived up to his nickname by preparing a feast of his own devising that was eagerly consumed. For some time they sat in silence, each cocooned in his own thoughts.

Now that time had given them chance to reflect on their recent undertakings, Nelson for one was wondering whether he had bitten off more than he could chew. The search for his uncle's legacy was proving far less straightforward than he had assumed when he first set out.

Glancing across the flickering tongues of flame at his partners, he smiled to himself. They were like chalk and cheese, but nevertheless imbued him with the confidence to face and overcome any pitfalls that life might throw in his path.

SIX

MOGOLLON

The following morning dawned bright and clear.
Dark rain clouds of the previous day had been
elbowed aside. The rising sun had sucked away any
wisps of mist still clinging to the valley floor.

First to rise, Chen Shing had scrambled above the
thick bottomland. Perched on a rocky ledge he
angled his gaze to the east, scanning every nook and
cranny for signs of pursuit. Nothing moved save for a
flock of quail heading south.

The little man's square jawline softened. His taut
muscles relaxed. It appeared as if they had once
again escaped retribution. Not that they had
anything to answer for. Black Jack had been the
offender, and his days as a cardsharp were
numbered.

Descending from his lofty vantage point, Chen
Shing returned to the camp where he was presented
with a plate of beans and fatback. It took a supreme

effort of will power to prevent his stubby nose from curling up in disgust. His Irish partner would most definitely not be on the blue ribbon list of premier cooks. Nonetheless Chen accepted the offering with good grace. Consumption of the repast was not so easily accomplished.

'Where Nelson?' he asked whilst pushing the loathsome food around his plate. 'He not sampling your breakfast?'

'Went off ten minutes since,' Riley smiled, shovelling down his own helping with gusto. 'Wanted seconds but I told him to hold off cos you hadn't eaten yet.' The Chinaman struggled to conceal a sour grimace as Riley added, 'He figured on getting in some gun practice.'

In confirmation, a succession of loud reports sang out from further along the draw.

Chen Shing put his empty plate down, grateful that his torment was at an end. Riley mistook the dwarf's sigh of relief for one of appreciation.

He moved across to the blackened pan beside the fire. 'Plenty more left,' he said digging a ladle into the congealed mess.

Chen Shing jumped to his feet. 'No! No!' he declared patting his belly. 'Me full to bursting.' Then his tiny legs scuttled towards the encircling ring of trees. 'Need to relieve self before setting off for Mogollon.'

'Glad you enjoyed the meal,' chirruped Riley. 'Next time, I'll give you a taste of real Irish stew.'

Luckily the gun shots drowned out the pained gurgle issuing from a Chinese maw.

The sun was already well above the scalloped moulding of the eastern horizon as the three riders guided their mounts back on to the main trail. Already the heat was making its presence felt.

Riley wiped his thick neck with a grubby bandanna. 'Gonna be another hot one.' he muttered.

Nobody disagreed.

But Nelson's thoughts were on more important notions than predicting the weather. He was contemplating the results of his shooting practice. Having used up two boxes of lead shot, he was well satisfied with the outcome. At first the tin cans had proved as elusive to pin down as a desert hare. Yet by the end of the session he was hitting half of them, and even his misses were not too far wide of the mark.

Practice makes perfect was clearly an adage with more than a ring of truth. And Chen Shing further boosted his confidence by quoting yet another of his learned ancestors' maxims: *Perseverance is a necessary ingredient of genius.*

Yes indeed, that was something towards which he would resolutely strive.

The journey to Mogollon was reckoned to be around five days. By noon of the second day out it was becoming patently obvious why the stagecoach terminated at Quemado. Nowhere was the trail more than six feet wide. And the tortuous nature of the route, twisting and curling like a giant serpent, would have made coach travel well nigh impossible. This was packmule country.

Boulders dislodged from their precarious perches

atop the canyon rims littered the rough terrain. Some almost as big as a house had to be circumnavigated. Narrow creeks bubbled and chattered as they careered down from the heights above, meandering at a more sedate pace as they hit the lower levels. This was where the precious yellow temptation would be most in evidence.

The trio knew they were getting close to Mogollon when they came across a scattering of small camps where men were ardently working their claims. Some preferred to work alone, not trusting the avaricious intentions of their associates. But operating alone was a slow and lonely process. Only through luck or a smattering of good fortune could a lone panner using a rocker ever hope to strike it rich.

Most gold-seekers were prepared to risk taking on partners for the much higher odds of hitting pay dirt in a big way. It also helped to while away the hours at the end of a hard day's graft.

Few miners even bothered to raise their heads as the riders passed by, so intent were they on sorting through the ore-bearing gravel for that all-important nugget that was to make them rich. And more prospectors meant less chance for the rest.

Heaps of sifted debris littered the creek bottomlands. Along with the discarded residue of human waste, the scene was one of utter despoliation. Many of the trees had been cut down to make log cabins and water flumes. A wasteland of bare trunks stretched halfway up both sides of the valley.

And the closer they got to Mogollon, the worse it

became. Roped-off claims hugged the banks of the tributaries, making it clear that the entire valley had been invaded. Not a single square inch of ground was immune from the scavengings of the gold-seekers.

Then they saw it.

Rows of off-white canvas tents lined the outer limits of the town. More permanent structures followed along the widening thoroughfare, bearing signs announcing the services available within. Haircutting, hardware and clothing establishments vied for position alongside the inevitable drinking and gambling dens.

The most important, however, as far as the miners were concerned was the assay office. The small square building always had a queue of excited men eagerly awaiting the pay-out from their claims.

Mogollon had first came to prominence in 1860. And now, a little over ten years later, a second discovery was resurrecting its fortunes. Many of the abandoned buildings along Fremont Street were receiving a much-needed facelift by incomers hoping to cash in on the new strike.

In six months the town had doubled in size. It was humming with activity. From dawn 'til dusk, there was a constant shift of men and materials between Mogollon and the goldfields.

Nelson's mouth hung askew.

So this was what a real boom town was like.

Joining the throng on Fremont Street, they were constantly jostled as wagons, horses and pack animals contributed to the mind-boggling turmoil. It was late afternoon, the busiest time of the day. Miners were returning from the diggings to do business in the town or register their discoveries; others were buying in new supplies for the next day.

A frenetic hubbub mingled with the stench of animal dung and blocked waste pipes. Nobody seemed to notice. All that mattered was the smell of gold. Only the snouts of newcomers twitched as the ever-present odours bit home.

Those miners on whom Lady Luck had recently smiled were hollering the loudest. They also attracted the most attention, both from hangers-on hoping to join in the celebrations and from those praying for the good fortune to rub off on them.

Riley pointed his cayuse to one of the few hitching rails that were unoccupied. The three riders tied off their mounts and stepped on to the wooden board-walk.

'Boys,' announced the Irishman with a deep sigh. 'I could sure use a drink.'

'Me too,' agreed Nelson. His mouth was drier than an engineer's glove.

Only the little Chinaman hung back.

'What's wrong, Chop Suey?' asked the Irishman, who was already shouldering through the batwings. 'We'll look out for you. Ain't nobody gonna tug at your pigtail while Mick Riley's around.'

The little guy sniffed the air.

'No like this place,' he said. The dark comment was accompanied by an uneasy shuffling. 'It give off bad vibrations. We should leave here now.'

'What you talkin' about? Not more of that

Oriental hocus-pocus,' scoffed Riley. 'We only just arrived.'

A trembling of the squat body was the sole reaction to the Irishman's ribbing. Nelson eyed his diminutive partner askance. He was not so quick to deride the Chinaman's intuition. The little guy's hunches had proved sound on all previous occasions.

'What our Irish friend is trying to say is' – Nelson gave his partner an admonitory look before continuing – 'Do you have any firm suspicions about Mogollon that we should know about?'

Chen Shing clasped his tiny hands together.

'Bad joss! Bad joss! I feel it in here.'

A clenched fist hammered at his heaving chest. The pudgy features had assumed a waxy pallor akin to that of a ripe banana. Large round eyes bulged in fear.

Ever the one to recognize distress in his fellow travellers, Nelson placed a comforting arm around the dwarf's twitching shoulders. Maybe it would be wise to heed the little man's trepidation.

'All right then. One drink only,' he decided, taking a middle course whilst holding Riley's gaze. Then he added with a brief chuckle: 'Just to clear the dust from our throats.' Turning back to Chen Shing, he said in a more serious vein: 'You go find us a place to bed down for the night. And I'll hunt out a pack-mule. Mick here can buy in enough supplies for a month. Just like we agreed over supper last night.'

He waited for nods of agreement from both men. Satisfied that the Chinaman had been sufficiently placated, he finished by adding, 'If that's all settled we'll be able to hit the trail at first light. Now for that drink.'

'I thought you'd never get round to it,' growled Riley, setting his hat at a jaunty angle as he shouldered through the jostling throng towards the bar.

'You come to pay what's owing, Driscoll?'

The question sounded more like a demand. It was aimed at an old dude clutching a battered hat and sporting a hangdog expression that clearly indicated to all those in the room that Abe Driscoll did not have the wherewithal to pay his debts.

'I need more time, Mr Garrison,' he pleaded. Then with a brief display of bravado, he spat. 'You ain't givin' us the chance to strike paydirt. I borrowed that dough on the understanding that we could settle up when a strike was made. I know there's gold in that creek. All the signs for a big hit are there. You just gotta give me the chance to prove it.'

Sitting behind a large mahogany desk, Diamond Jim Garrison's beady eyes gleamed avariciously. With casual ease he snipped the end off a fat cigar and stuck it between his teeth. Instantly a lackey standing to one side sprang forward and applied a lighted match.

Exuding a lordly air of self-assurance, Diamond Jim fingered his trademark stick pin, knowing he was in control and had the whip hand. His florid visage broke into an oily smile. But there was no trace of humour behind the crystalline blue eyes, only a cold, implacable resolve to bring the meeting to a rapid finale.

This was the third such foreclosure he had undertaken in the month since he had set up shop in Mogollon. With vast numbers of miners flooding into the town, many seeking a grubstake, he was confident it would not be the last.

At first it had been Garrison's intention merely to occupy one of the numerous empty stores in the town and stock it with the equipment he had shipped out from Leavenworth.

Ever the astute and unscrupulous businessman, he had quickly observed that there was more money to be made by tricking naïve prospectors out of their claims by initiating his own dubious mining contracts. Supported by a bunch of hard-nosed toughs, Diamond Jim envisaged a prosperous sojourn for himself in Mogollon. The future looked rosy. Indeed, he might even be able to retire in a year to one of those Mexican haciendas he had seen on the outskirts of Santa Fe.

The shuffling heap of untidy rags on the far side of the desk returned his thoughts to the current business of securing another claim.

'You signed a contract to return the stake I loaned you within three weeks.' The statement was delivered in a flat monotone devoid of feeling. Charity and forbearance were not in Garrison's nature.

Abe Driscoll's jaw dropped.

'There weren't no mention of any three damn weeks when you agreed to help me out,' snapped the prospector. His gnarled features were twisted with anger. Garrison gave a nonchalant shrug of his broad shoulders.

'You miners are all the same,' he quipped. 'You should have read the small print. It's all there in black and white.' Then his voice hardened to a brittle rasp. 'Now pay up, or hand over the deeds to your claim.'

The trader's bodyguards stiffened, their hands flexing. They were ready, just in case the old guy made any stupid move.

'You heard the boss,' cut in a tall hardcase dressed in black. From the top of his high-crowned Stetson down to his polished boots, Randy Quail oozed menace that was backed up by the twin-holstered gun rig that was clearly not for idle display. 'Now cut the excuses and make your choice.'

'Why, you no-good bunch of chisellers,' railed Driscoll. The veins in his scrawny neck pulsed and throbbed like fat worms. He was good and mad. 'You're only in Mogollon to cheat hard-working miners out of their poke. Well it ain't gonna happen to me.'

Driscoll went for his pistol. But it snagged on his belt. Before he could drag it free, Randy Quail had effortlessly palmed his own hogleg. With a smirk of derision, the hardass shot the miner without a moment's hesitation.

Blood pumped from the chest wound as Driscoll staggered backwards under the brutal impact of the heavy slug. He sank to his knees, head lolling, then keeled over, dead.

For the first time Garrison lumbered to his feet. He stepped round the desk. Roughly he searched the old man's clothing for the all-important contract and claim certificate.

A lurid grin split his face as he snatched the documents from an inside pocket. His nose wrinkled in disgust at the grizzly spectacle now staining his new carpet.

Addressing an undersized runt idly leaning on a Kentucky rifle and puffing on a smelly corncob, he snapped, 'Get this heap of garbage out of here, Coonskin. Its making the place look untidy.'

Randy Quail sniggered dutifully as Coonskin Lamaar hurriedly shuffled forward. The thin weasel was clad in dirty buckskins and boasted a straggly grey moustache. Perched on his thatch of lank grey hair was the ever-present ringtailed fur cap.

'Sure thing, boss,' Lamaar replied. He was assisted by a burly sidekick appropriately named Stony Cragg. Unceremoniously, the pair of roughnecks manhandled the cadaver over to the door.

'And make sure you dump it well away from here,' added Garrison. 'We don't want the vigilance committee sniffing around.'

SEVEN

ALARMING NEWS

It was the brightly painted gold and blue sign that attracted Mick Riley's attention. Just as it was meant to do. In time the paint would fade just like that of all the other mercantiles along Freemont Street.

Mogollon General Goods Emporium – If it ain't here, it don't exist.

A confident assertion. But the proprietor knew exactly what sort of goods his customers would be seeking. Most if not all were miners, their entire world being centred around the gold just itching to be scooped up from the tumbling creek beds close to Mogollon. Diamond Jim Garrison had been in their position once and knew exactly what goods they would be seeking. And it was his intention to supply them – at a price!

The store was a large double-fronted establishment.

Inside, Riley paused to imbibe the smells and

absorb the goods on offer. A couple of young sprogs were buying carpentry tools. They were clearly intending to erect a cabin. One of them grudgingly handed over a heap of greenbacks. The Irishman couldn't help but overhear the terse reaction spat out by his sidekick.

'For that price we could have bought sawn lumber as well as tools back in Santa Fe.'

The clerk's response was equally curt. He had heard it all before.

'Then you should have brought it with you. Now, if there's nothing else?' His beaky snout gave a supercilious twitch of disdain. The two greenhorns grumbled incoherently but knew they had no choice but to accept the fact that in the frontier boom towns, it was a seller's market. After grabbing up their purchases the sulky pair shuffled over to the door.

'You'll be a-smirking' on the other side of that rat-assed face of your'n when we strike it rich,' growled the smaller prospector, hitching up his loose corduroy pants before slamming out on to the boardwalk.

Beaky sniffed, then turned to address the newcomer.

'Can I help you?' His manner was no less haughty with Riley.

With some effort the feisty Irishman managed to contain his natural instinct to floor this smarmy dude. Having been obliged to consume only a single glass of beer at the saloon, he made no adverse comment, merely handing over the list of supplies.

It was extensive. They would be trekking into

remote territory where few people had previously ventured.

Beyond Mogollon, what passed for civilization terminated abruptly. All the mining encampments were concentrated to the south. Westward, there were no towns, only the vague possibility of isolated trading posts. Any trails they encountered would be little more than animal runs.

The trio would be well and truly on their own.

The clerk's thick eyebrows lifted. His previous hauteur vanished, the oily vocals assuming a more accommodating vein.

'This is a big order, mister,' he murmured, studying the list. 'It'll take me a couple of hours to prepare.' Then his hooded eyes narrowed, the thin lips compressed in a tight line. 'You gotten the means to pay?'

Riley smiled. He dug into the saddle-bag slung over his shoulder and removed a small leather pouch which he then shook. The contents jingled merrily.

'Would that be answering your question, then?' The lyrical Irish cadence was deliberately exagerated.

The clerk immediately became sycophantic, rubbing his hands.

'Of course, sir,' he fawned nodding his hawklike skull. 'I will get on with it straight away.'

Now it was Riley's turn to assume a lofty air.

'See that it be all ready for loading on to our mules in two hours.' He held the unctuous toady with a cool glare. 'I'll be back at' – he flipped out a silver pocket watch from his vest pocket and purposefully studied the dial, omitting to inform the clerk that it had ceased to operate the previous week – 'at five o'clock.'

'Certainly, sir,' repeated the clerk, then asked in a rather tentative tone, 'Are you heading up country, then?'

'Me and my partners have information that. . . .' Just in time, Riley stopped himself, realizing that in a place like Mogollon the slightest hint of a new discovery, however remote, could lead to inconvenient problems they could well do without. 'We are heading into Arizona on a hunting trip.'

At that moment the sharp crack of a handgun came from the room above the store.

'What was that?' rapped the Irishman, snatching at the rosewood handle of the .31 Whitney revolver slung round his waist.

The clerk was quick to allay any fears. He shrugged his narrow shoulders. 'Probably just one of the boys upstairs potting varmints out the back lot. Happens all the time.'

Riley grunted, settled his nerves, then made for the door. Passing a jar of stiped candy, he hooked out a stick and popped it into his mouth. His raised eye met that of the storekeeper.

'On the house, sir.'

Riley nodded. 'Five o'clock. On the dot.'

The door closed behind him.

As he walked along, sucking on the sweet comestible, the multiplicity of street noises passed him by. The crack of a bullwhip, the squeaking sign, the harsh clatter of rolling stock – all went unheeded.

Consequently, he failed to notice a young woman hurrying towards him along the boardwalk. Her mind was also on other things. The deep frown-lines creasing her forehead indicated that her thoughts were anything but pleasant. Indeed, to those who might have noticed, she appeared to be extremely worried.

A collision was inevitable.

Packages that the woman had been carrying were strewn across the walkway. Riley's candy ended up poking out of a muddy pool in the street. Both were taken aback by the unexpected incident.

Riley was the first to recover. Apologizing profusely, he picked up the array of packages. Being a red-blooded Irishman, he couldn't help noticing that beneath the rough work-clothes, there dwelt a comely female. Even the denim overalls failed to hide the svelte figure.

'It's sorry I am to have been so clumsy,' he gushed, red-faced, trying to hide his embarrassment. 'Not looking where I was going.'

The woman quickly recovered her composure. Removing her slouch hat, she bowed in acknowledgement. Titian hair cascaded down over her shoulders.

Riley's mouth fell open.

'Apology accepted,' the woman replied with a smile that lit up her radiant face.

For the moment, her problems had taken a back seat. Nobody paid any attention to the encounter. Such was the nature of a mining camp where the search for gold took precedence over all else. Riley's chivalrous gesture was like a ray of sunshine.

She couldn't help noticing that the Irishman had just emerged from the Mogollon General Goods Emporium. 'Have you been in the store?' she said, concern tightening the smooth jawline.

He nodded, waiting for her to continue, content to just ogle this lustrous vision that had tumbled into his life.

'Was there an old man in there?' she asked. The frown had intensified as the woman's anxiety reasserted itself. 'Tall and thin with silver hair.'

Riley shook his head.

'Just me, and two young guys after setting up a claim.' Only now did he take note of the woman's distressed state. 'Was he a friend of yours?'

'My father,' she said. 'He should have finished his business with Jim Garrison by now.'

The storekeeper's name jerked Riley out of his dreamy ruminations. 'Garrison, you say?' The snappy retort took the girl by surprise.

'You know him?'

'That I do,' prickled the Irishman. 'Diamond Jim Garrison. Here in Mogollon.' The name emerged from his throat as a gruff croak. 'Never figured to meet up with him again. If ever a more black-hearted critter walked God's earth, then I have yet to encounter such a specimen.'

'How do you know him?'

'To be sure it's a long story. Me and my buddies have a score to settle with that gent.'

'Then I can only advise you to watch your step,' warned the young woman, clutching at his knotty arm. 'He's crafty as a sidewinder and twice as deadly. Always has a bunch of hard-nosed bodyguards to look after his scurvy hide. And he never leaves the office above the store without protection.'

'Judging by the prices he charges, I can understand why,' replied Riley. 'So what's the scabby knave done to cause you offence?'

'We owe him money that he loaned us for setting up our claim. Now he wants it back. But we haven't had chance to work the claim properly yet. Pa was going to plead our case. But I'm worried he'll lose his temper if Garrison refuses to give us more time.' Her eyes filled with tears. But she held them in check, not wishing to unburden herself to a stranger.

That was when Riley remembered the single gunshot above the store. He struggled to prevent the tightness around his mouth revealing the concern he now felt for the old prospector's safety. Attempting to lighten the young woman's sombre mood, he offered a jaunty quip.

'Even now your pa could be celebrating 'cos of the reprieve he's won. Mark my words. He'll be in some saloon downing a few beers.'

'You really think so?' She quickly latched on to Riley's optimstic attitude. After all, what other alternative was there? 'I'll have another wander round town.'

'I'm sure he'll turn up. Although in what state, I ain't so sure.'

She laughed. It emerged more like a choked gurgle as she gathered up the packages. They shook hands.

'Much obliged for your kindness,' she said. 'My name is Emma Driscoll.'

'Mick Riley,' responded the big Irishman whose beefy paw enfolded the girl's tiny hand. 'If I come across your pa, I'll keep tabs on him.'

After thanking him, she disappeared. A vision of loveliness lost amidst the heaving throng of Freemont Street.

Garrison was locking the Driscoll documents in his wall safe when the door burst open. Instantly three guns were pointing at the intruder. But it was only Chet Bradley, the store clerk. The bodyguards relaxed, easing back the cocked hammers on their pistols.

'You could get yourself drilled full of lead entering a room without knocking,' railed Garrison with a disdainful sneer.

'Just thought you ought to know, boss.' Bradley paused staring down the gun barrels and suddenly realizing how close he had come to meeting his Maker. Beads of sweat bubbled on his forehead.

'Well?' snapped Garrison peevishly, whilst adjusting his silk necktie. 'What's so all-fired important that sees you leaving the store unattended?'

'There was an Irish guy in the store buying up a pile of supplies. Money no object.'

'So?'

'You told me to spill the lowdown about anybody I reckoned was on to a good deal.' Bradley's confidence was returning. He sat down. 'Well, this dude seemed too damned sure of himself. I figure he knows the whereabouts of a fresh strike.'

'What makes you so sure of this?'

The clerk relaxed knowing he now had the boss's attention. This could earn him a hefty bonus in his next pay packet.

'Soon as I questioned him he let slip about certain information that had come his way. Then he clammed up and burbled some'n about him and his partners heading west on a hunting trip.'

'Yeah!' scoffed Quail as he deftly rolled a stogie. 'And the moon's made of green cheese.'

'That's right,' agreed Garrison, his sneering features a granite mask. 'Anybody heading west of this dump must have the yellow stuff on their minds.'

'What we gonna do, boss?' enquired Bradley.

Garrison said nothing. His piercing gaze was glassy and distant as he considered this new development. Randy Quail and the storekeeper waited expectantly.

Just then, Coonskin Lamaar and Stony Cragg returned from having dumped their grisly burden.

Garrison ignored them. But when he eventually came to a decision it was Lamaar whom he addressed. Being of a small and wiry stature, he was the only one of Garrison's men suitable for the task the trader had in mind.

'Got another job for you, Coonskin,' he said. 'Something that should be just up your street.'

Lamaar was all ears.

'There's an Irish jigger newly arrived in town. I want you to find out where the guy's staying and search his room. I need to know the intentions of him and his partners. Chet here will give you a description. Think you can manage it?'

'Sure thing, boss,' chirped the little guy, making for the door.

'And don't get caught!' rapped Garrison fixing him with a warning grimace. 'Leave it until after midnight when the town's settled down.'

'Quieter than a shadow, that's me,' piped Lamaar. 'That bogtrotter won't know a thing about it.'

Emma Driscoll was more than a little anxious. Her father was nowhere to be found. She had paid a visit to all his usual haunts without success. Nobody had seen him.

Completely at a loss and becoming ever more frantic by the minute, she had decided to take the bull by the horns and pay Jim Garrison a visit. He was her last hope. Even if he didn't know the whereabouts of her father, at least she would find out exactly how his meeting with the cunning trader had gone.

Hustling into the store, she ignored the clerk's blustering protestations and stamped up the stairs. Her normally seraphic features were set hard as cement as she slammed through the office door unannounced.

Ever the professional gunslinger, Randy Quail had both his revolvers out in a flash, the hammers drawn back to full cock.

Garrison's unsettled frown softened as soon as he realized that no immediate danger threatened. He uttered a blithe chuckle.

'Its all right, Randy. No need for gunplay where

Miss Driscoll is concerned.' Garrison resumed his seat, gently rocking to and fro as a lascivious gleam appraised the young woman's admirable contours. 'To what do I owe this most welcome visit?'

Now that her father was out of the picture, Jim Garrison figured it would be a good notion to muscle in on a far more sensous claim. Kill two birds with one stone, so to speak.

Emma saw the lustful glint washing across the trader's smarmy visage. And she was having none of it.

Ignoring the unctuous charm, she rapped, 'Where is my father?'

Garrison's broad shoulders lifted in a casual shrug.

'He came here to settle some business regarding the claim,' pressed the girl undeterred.

'Have you seen Mr Driscoll?' Garrison addressed the query to Randy Quail who was once again lolling against the wall cleaning his fingernails with a small knife.

'He left here over an hour ago,' replied the gunslinger without looking up from his task.

'So what was the outcome of the meeting?'

Garrison gave an exaggerated lift of his eyebrows.

'The claim, what was decided?' persisted the woman impatiently. Garrison made no pretence of concealing a sly grin as he detected her icy demeanour beginning to crack. 'Are you going to give us more time to pay?'

'I think that is a matter you should discuss with your father,' answered the trader. 'After all, it is his signature on the agreement.'

'You won't tell me anything then?' Emma was fast losing her cool.

Garrison merely returned her angry glare with one of naïve innocence.

Emma turned on her heels and left, to avoid giving the ogling toad the satisfaction of witnessing her anguish.

'Always be assured, Miss Driscoll,' called Garrison after her disappearing back. 'Any time you wish to call on my help, the door will always be open.'

Undisguised sniggers from the trader's body-guards followed her down the stairs. Fearing the worst, Emma decided that she would have to call on the doctor to see if he had any news of her father's disappearance.

Heart thumping under her ribs, the woman's pace slowed to a crawl as she approached the surgery. Tentatively she knocked on the door.

As soon as the sawbones perceived the identity of his caller she knew that her worst fears had been realized. He could not hide the grim cast that only the direst of tidings could produce.

'I'm sorry, my dear,' he blurted out inadequately. There was nothing more to say as he led her inside and through to the back room which was used as a mortuary. A body was laid out on a marble slab and covered with a white shroud.

Emma's face was ashen as she raised the sheet. A choking gurgle stuck in her throat on beholding the corpse that was her father. Tears flowed down her blotched cheeks.

'A drunk found him on a vacant lot behind the

livery stable,' said the medic, placing a comforting hand on her shoulder. 'If you would like to be left alone. . . ?'

The woman nodded absently.

It was an hour later as she was riding back to the claim that Emma Driscoll began to suspect a connection between her father's death and Diamond Jim Garrison. But what proof had she? None.

EIGHT

UNWELCOME VISITOR

When Nelson was informed by his Irish partner that
Diamond Jim Garrison was in Mogollon, a red mist
immediately clouded his reasoning. The news had
knocked the stuffing out of him. The rat was
supposed to be heading back east to Leavenworth.
Once recovered, he was all for storming over to the
store that very minute to settle the matter in
company with his new pistol. Not even Riley's perti-
nent revelation that Garrison had surrounded
himself with a gang of hard-boiled gun-slicks was
going to dent his resolve.

Nelson had leapt to his feet and was buckling on
his gunbelt.

'That bastard needs a dose of his own medicine,'
he ranted, grabbing his hat and purposefully setting
it straight on his head. 'I never thought a chance to

79

get even like this would offer itself. And now that it has, I aim to take full advantage.' He checked that the Navy Colt was fully loaded, then hustled over to the door of his hotel room where the three gold seekers had congregated.

Once again it was the restraining influence of Chen Shing that sought to calm him down. The little man scampered across to block the doorway.

'Out of the way, Chen,' rasped Nelson towering over the diminutive Chinaman. The situation had the appearance of a music hall parody but there was no humour in Nelson's terse statement. 'No way am I letting that son of Satan off the hook now that we've caught up with him,' he hissed.

'This no time to lose head in search of revenge,' said Chen Shing in a low yet firm voice, whilst maintaining his stance. His fervent gaze held that of his fiery confederate, willing his friend to see sense. 'Mick is right. You no match for hired gunmen. Only get self killed.'

The Chinaman's insistent reasoning was hard to gainsay.

'I don't know,' Nelson muttered, still not fully convinced.

Chen pressed home his attack, perceiving that his young buddy's belligerent attitude was wavering.

'As American proverb say, there are more ways than one to skin a rabbit.'

'Ain't that the goldarned truth?' Riley smiled with a touch of attitude. 'We can allus come back and do the job properly at a time of our own choosing. Once your uncle's hidden loot has been found, we can hire a small army to cook Garrison's goose once and for all. Bursting in there now is sure to end in tears.' He placed a comradely arm around his young partner's shoulder. 'And it ain't likely to be Garrison that'll be blubbing.'

Nelson hesitated.

But the red curtain was beginning to part. Use of the term 'we' by the Irishman warmed Nelson's heart. It made him feel closer than ever to his new companions. It also proved they were true *amigos*, that they were in this venture to the finish, howsoever that might turn out in the final analysis.

What Chen Shing and Riley had asserted made good sense. And with Garrison in Mogollon, backed up by a gang of hardened rough necks, it would only be a matter of time before their presence was uncovered. Then the fat would certainly be in the fire.

There was only one reasonable course of action to be taken.

The sooner they left for the Natanes Plateau and Bronco Canyon the better.

'What do you say, then, if we pull out at first light?' suggested Nelson, allowing himself to be led over to a seat. Riley stuck a glass of whiskey in his hand. The raw spirit served to further drive out the pugnacious demons that had been ravaging his mind.

'The wise man chooses his own field of battle.' The dwarf nodded sagely.

The two white men offered each other a wry smile. Then they all clinked glasses and toasted the future.

Sanity and good judgement had once again taken charge.

Evening shadows had surrendered their tenuous grip on the day by the time this conclusion had been reached. Outside in the street the tinkling of a piano and raucous laughter from a myriad throats informed the three *compadres* that it was time to hit the sack if an early departure was to be made.

Riley had no idea how long he had been asleep. But something vague and indeterminate registered on the fringes of his consciousness. His eyes opened. Quickly he shrugged off the soporific lethargy, then lay there in the darkness struggling to work out what had disturbed him.

'Who's there?' he burbled, still half-asleep.

A scuffling on the far side of the room impinged itself on his turgid brain cells. It was accompanied by a hazy shift of movement, instantly stilled by the shaky holler.

But not for long.

The shadow came suddenly, taking Riley by surprise. At first it had been nothing more than an opaque blot that caught his eye. Then it assumed more of the physical, taking on movement, swift and terminal, as it lunged towards him.

Instinct more than anything else found Riley flinging himself sideways as his ears picked up the lethal whisper cutting through the air.

He glimpsed a thin shaft of light. The knife struck the iron bedstead, a paper's width from his tense body. Luckily for Riley, the solid impact dragged the weapon from the intruder's grasp. With a desperation born out of pure survival, the Irishman rolled out of the bed and on to the hard floor. Now wide awake, he leapt to his feet in a smoothly adroit flow of movement.

But the interloper was not to be thwarted that easily. A growl emerged from the gloom as he came in lunging wildly at the Irishman's hazy outline.

'Stupid bogtrotter. You shouldn't have woken up.'

The guy was quick as a rattler's tongue. In and out, one blow colliding with Riley's shoulder, the other slamming into his cheek.

'Aaaaagh!'

A pained croak disgorged from the big Irishman's throat as he tottered backwards. Reaching out a hand for support, he quickly shook the stunning effects from his head. A sickly chortle penetrated his brain when he realized that the man had retrieved his blade and was preparing for another attack.

But this time Riley was ready.

He sidestepped the swinging slash, ducking low and driving a bunched fist into the guy's stomach. A whoosh of air expelled from the open mouth. The killer staggered back clutching at his midriff, the lethal knife slithering from his grasp on to the floor with a metallic thud.

Realizing the initiative had swung in his opponent's favour, the assailant made a grab at the water jug on the dresser and flung it at Riley's advancing profile. The Irishman parried the heavy pot aside, sending it crashing into the wall.

But the delaying tactics were sufficient to enable the rat to escape. By the time Riley had reached the door, he was nowhere to be seen. Pounding feet on the outside stairway of the hotel told him the direction to take. Without thought, he took off after his quarry. But he was too late. Horse and rider were soon lost amidst the Stygian gloom of the back lot.

'What's all that ruckus about?'

Nelson had emerged from his own room, immediately followed by Chen Shing. Other residents stuck their heads out into the corridor, grumbling about the disturbance to their slumbers.

Down in the lobby the clock struck three.

'Nothing to worry about, folks.' The assurance came from Mick Riley as he stifled the heavy breathing occasioned by his traumatic ordeal. 'Just a bunch of late revellers on their way home.' He had no wish to broadcast the failed attack to all and sundry. With calm deliberation he ushered the guests back into their rooms. Then he signalled for his partners to join him.

Splashing a double measure of whiskey into a glass he sank the hard liquor in a single draught, gasping as the raw spirit burned a passage down into his stomach. Having recovered his composure, the Irishman quickly outlined the nature of the break in.

Chen Shing picked up the discarded knife. In his small hands it resembled a cavalry sabre.

'A near thing,' he sighed, hefting the ugly weapon. 'You one lucky feller.'

'Don't I know it.' Riley examined the discoloured bruise on his right cheek in the mirror, wincing as clumsy fingers probed the tender injury. It could have been a lot worse if he hadn't awoken in time.

Then he went on, 'Seems to me like this is Garrison's doing.'

'He hasn't wasted any time,' remarked Nelson. 'You figure he knows we're in town already?'

'I wouldn't put anything past that skunk,' snarled Riley.

'Any notion as to what he was after?'

Riley's colourful features hardened.

'Garrison probably has spies all over town reporting on any newcomers that arrive. I was buying a heap of supplies from his store. A bit of a coincidence, don't you think, that on the very same night, my room receives an unwelcome visitor? So I don't figure it was any ordinary break-in.' He responded to Nelson's quizzical frown by adding, 'The rat knew I was Irish. And he was most definitely looking for something. It was only when I challenged him that he tried to pin me to the bed with that thing.' He nodded at the glinting weapon held by Chen Shing.

'In one way it's a blessing it was you who bought the supplies,' cogitated Nelson, sipping at his drink. 'That meant it was your room he broke into.'

'How d'yuh figure that then?' parried the rather disgruntled Irishman, once again probing his injured face. 'I may be a thick-headed bogtrotter, but that don't mean I enjoy getting slugged all over the place.'

'You got me wrong,' mollified Nelson. 'I'm a heavier sleeper than you.'

'So?' queried a puzzled Mick Riley.

'So the thief could have easily gone through my things undisturbed and found the map and directions to the hidden stash.'

Riley sat up, mouth agape as the logic of Nelson's reasoning dawned.

'Well, he not come back again tonight now game has been rumbled,' cut in the dwarf. 'But only a fool places his head in the lion's mouth.'

Concurring with the little man's eloquent sagacity, an owl hooted in accord. All three now realized that Mogollon was not a healthy place in which to linger.

'That's it then,' announced Nelson, hurriedly draining his glass and standing up. 'Time to make ourselves scarce. I don't see how he could have rumbled Uncle Jeb's discovery. But this isn't the time to play around with snakes.' The young gold-seeker set about gathering his things together. 'As you so eloquently pointed out, Chop Suey, we can always scupper Garrison's game once the lucre is safely in our hands.'

And so it was agreed.

The other two returned to their own rooms in preparation for making a surreptitious and rapid exit from Mogollon.

Within the hour the stealthy trio were heading east out of town towards the imposing foothills of the Tularosas. Once beyond the town limits they were soon forced into single file on a little-used trail no wider than a portly hog. It was a stroke of good fortune that just then the moon elected to assist their progress by shrugging aside a band of stifling cloud. Even so, the heavily laden pack mules ensured that the fastest pace they could muster was little more than a gentle trot.

A silvery glow, hauntingly mesmeric, bathed the landscape. The appearance was strangely akin to that of a winter wonderland. Save for their own strained progress driven on by the fear of pursuit, nothing moved.

After a half-hour, Nelson signalled a halt. He cocked an ear to their back trail, listening intently.

A comforting silence, broken only by the familiar creak of saddle leather, enfolded them in its welcoming embrace.

Satisfied they were not being followed, Nelson spurred ahead.

Gradually the nature of the terrain began to change as the trail entered a loose scattering of ponderosa pine. With the gradient becoming ever sharper, the tree cover closed about the three riders and their packmules. Nothing was able to penetrate the dense overhead canopy. Deprived of moonlight, the small party were forced down to an unremitting plod up the serpentine trail.

Eventually they emerged on to an open plateau just as the genesis of the new day was emerging. Streaks of pink and yellow elbowed aside the grey dawn to reveal a starkly austere landscape. On all sides fractured buttresses of orange sandstone interspersed with desiccated juniper had replaced the thick cloak of pine forest.

As undisputed leader of the expedition, Nelson had maintained a steady pace throughout the hours of darkness. Although anxious to place as much distance as possible between themselves and

Diamond Jim Garrison, on more than one occasion he had almost fallen out of the saddle due to tiredness.

Having enjoyed little sleep since the previous night, he realized they all desperately needed a rest to avoid a serious accident frustrating their plans. And with the sun peeping above the eastern rim of the mountains, he was now able to look out for a suitable campsite.

NINE

HOLED UP!

Coonskin Lamaar was sweating. And it had nothing to do with the rapidly strengthening sun. His failure to discover anything in the Irishman's room, not to mention the ignominious exit on the run, had shaken him up. He had delayed a meeting with Garrison for as long as possible. The boss was not going to be well pleased.

But, save for quitting Mogollon, he had no other choice than to face the music. And this was a good job, easy money. So far!

Garrison was seated at the rear of the Golden Goose saloon enjoying a slap-up breakfast in his favourite booth. It faced on to the front door so that he could observe everybody who entered, so averting any chance of his being surprised. A man in his position could not afford to take any unneccesary risks.

He had been expecting a visit from Lamaar. The shifty turd was late. Garrison was forking a chunk of bacon into his mouth as the little weasel eventually plucked up the courage to enter the gloomy interior of the saloon.

The trader's face hardened. He could smell a failed operation a mile off. And Lamaar's furtive manner was a dead give-away.

'What have you got for me?' he snapped out as the little guy sidled up to the table.

Lamaar shuffled his feet, the melancholic expression measurably deepening.

'Well?' hissed Garrison.

'I tried, boss.' Lamaar whined, 'but the guy must have been awake.'

'So you failed,' the gang boss shot back, the piercing glower from his black eyes skewering Lamaar to the wall. 'A simple job like that and you couldn't manage it. He and his sidekicks will be on their guard from now on. I oughta blast you here and now.' A minuscule Springfield .28 pocket revolver had leapt into his palm. The barrel was pointing at Lamaar's quivering lips. Seconds passed. To the little hardcase it seemed like an hour.

Then, a mirthless smile split Garrison's tight features.

'I'll give you one more chance.'

'Anything, boss. You just name it.'

Garrison dabbed some egg yolk from his thick lips with a napkin before proceeding while Lamaar nervously fingered the tail of his coonskin hat.

'The Driscoll girl.' A brief yet mordant pause followed as Garrison carefully eyed his employee. 'She's gonna cause us big trouble. So I want her out of the picture. With her pa dead and the claim in my hands, she's gonna suspect I'm behind it. And I don't want the vigilance committee sticking their noses into my affairs. Any lawyer worth his salt will soon realize those contracts are worthless.'

'Don't worry, boss,' chimed Lamaar eagerly. 'I won't fail you this time.'

'You better not,' hissed Garrison, giving the pistol a suggestive tap. As an afterthought he went on, 'Maybe you should take Stony with you as back-up?'

Coonskin drew himself up to his full height of five foot six.

'I don't need that knucklehead to hold my hand,' he scoffed.

The gang leader grimaced.

'Just make sure it looks like an accident,' was his final blunt instruction as he resumed his interrupted meal.

Emma Driscoll was frightened.

She had ridden hard back to the claim on the banks of Happy Dan Creek and spent the rest of the day wondering what the future held. All along the tortuous length of the shallow draw other miners went about their daily grind of shovelling and sifting the raw gravel.

Emma just sat on the banks staring into the silvery flow. Idly she thought about the first miner to strike paydirt in the tributary valley. Dan Smollens had certainly left a happy man. Only a handful who had followed were so lucky. Abe Driscoll had expected to be one of the select few. Now he was just a memory.

As far as Emma was concerned, Happy Dan Creek was a sad and mournful place. There was no future here now.

Nobody appeared to notice her distraught frame of mind, nor cared. Gold was all that mattered. All alone in a hostile world dominated by gold-hungry men, the precarious nature of her situation struck home with a vengeance.

And it was that night when ghoulish thoughts of what might befall a young woman surged to the fore. Terrifying visions of her father's pale death mask were a haunting reminder of what her own fate could be. All night she tossed and turned. Eventually dropping off to sleep in the early hours, she was rudely awakened by the dreadful image of Diamond Jim Garrison's leering visage staring down at her comatose form.

A scream rent the static air. She struggled upright, an icy shiver prickling her spine. Then she sank back, thankful it was only a nightmare. But the feeling that the gang boss might already be planning her own violent demise caused the girl to break out in a cold sweat. Even now he could be heading this way to claim his ill-gotten gains.

Never having been prone to hysterical outbursts, Emma quickly brought her nerves under control. If Garrison thought she was a weak-willed female and an easy pushover, he was in for a rude awakening.

But what could she do?

Stepping outside the tent that had been her home for the last month, she paced along the creek bottom racking her brains for a solution. It was her arrival at the deep hole excavated by her father in his search for the elusive motherlode that suggested an answer to her dilemma.

A glint appeared in her eye.

Quickly she dismantled the tent and repositioned it in front of the hole. It was ten feet deep. With infinite care, she laid a spare tarpaulin cover over the top, pinning the corners with rocks. As a final touch to the charade, sand was sprinkled over the canvas. In the dark, it blended perfectly into the surrounding terrain.

A grim smile played across her smoothly aquiline features. Illuminated by the stark moonlight, it gave her a sinister, almost spectral presence.

Anyone who tried to take Emma Driscoll by surprise was in for an impressive reception. The hole had sheer walls so there was no way a bushwhacker could escape in a hurry. At least then she would know the score; that Diamond Jim Garrison wanted rid of her so he could operate the claim for his own gain.

If, by sun-up, no attempt had been made to evict her, then she would review the situation. But Emma was convinced in her own mind that Garrison would make his move before then.

Much as she would have preferred to remain and fight for her rights, she was a realist. A woman on her own had no chance of succeeding in a rough and ready mining town such as Mogollon. Her only hope was to get out while she was still able. Maybe at some later date, when proper law and order came to this remote outpost, she could return and seek justice for her father's murder.

But until then. . . .

After brewing a pot of coffee, she hung an oil lamp outside the tent as a guide for any would-be assailant to home into. Then she settled down. It was going to be a long night.

An hour later, her eyes were drooping with fatigue. Even the stimulating effect of the strong coffee was insufficient to keep her senses alert. The gun she had been holding slipped from her fingers. And, head lolling on her swanlike neck, she fell into a dreamless sleep.

How long Emma had been in the arms of Morpheus she had no way of knowing. It was a strident clamour outside the tent that brought her awake. The trap had been sprung.

She grabbed the lantern and hurried outside, peering down into the shadowed depths. A groan issued from the bowels of the pit. She instantly recognized the mousey profile of Coonskin Lamaar, one of Garrison's thugs.

Now she knew the truth.

There was no chance of Lamaar escaping from the hole unaided. Nevertheless, there could be others following in his wake. And they could arrive at any moment. All Emma's belongings had been packed the previous evening for just such an eventuality as this.

The tent was too cumbersome to take and would have to be abandoned. Not that Emma was unduly perturbed. As a gold prospector's daughter, she was used to camping out under the stars.

She mounted her fully laden horse and gazed

down at the recumbent form in the hole. Her lips compressed into a thin line.

'Tell your boss he can have the claim . . . for now.'

Emma cut short her invective. The emotive manner of her departure had suddenly threatened to overflow. Tears welled in her eyes. Her bosom heaved as palpitating shudders convulsed her slender frame. It took a considerable effort to bring herself under control before she felt able to continue. 'And make certain you remind Garrison that this is not the last he's heard from Emma Driscoll. Next time we meet, I'll be waving him good-bye at his very own necktie party.'

She could have said a lot more. But what was the point. Aiming a gobbet of spittle at the muttering figure, she spurred off.

Happy Dan Creek lay a good five miles to the west of Mogollon. She could not head towards the town for fear of meeting Garrison and his gang.

The only alternative lay to the west.

In fact it was around mid-afternoon of that day when Diamond Jim accompanied by Randy Quail, Stony Cragg and three other equally hard-nosed rannigans set out for Happy Dan Creek.

Throughout the morning Garrison had been growing ever more inflamed. By noon, he was like a bear with a sore head, snapping at his cohorts on the slightest pretext. And the whiskey bottle was receiving more than a passing glance.

'That chuckle-headed asshole should have been back hours ago,' he complained angrily for the umpteenth time, adding: 'Surely one girl on her own can't cause him that much trouble.'

Nobody proffered any comment. When the boss was in this frame of mind, it was best to keep a low profile. It was Randy Quail who eventually plucked up the nerve to suggest they rode out to the mining claim to suss out the situation. Garrison had been thinking along similar lines.

The Driscoll claim was located on the inside of a bend in the creek close to where another, smaller tributary joined in. The flat terrace between the two watercourses was an ideal spot for placer mining, and one reason that Garrison had decided to grubstake the old-timer. He was anxious to clear the area of its unwanted tenant so as to put his own men on to working the claim.

Cresting a low rise, the group of riders hauled rein. Keen eyes surveyed the creek bottom for any sign of life.

Apart from a trio of prairie dogs playing chase, the site appeared empty. A low breeze riffled the line of cottonwoods fronting the creek. In the distance other miners were going about the unending task of digging and filtering the paydirt. But close by, there was no sign of the girl, or Coonskin Lamaar.

The two tents were still there. Although it seemed strange that one was sited immediately in front of a large hole.

Garrison's thick eyebrows met in a puzzled frown.

'What do you make of that, Randy?' he asked his second-in-command pointing at the odd arrangement.

'Beats me, boss.'

'Maybe old Driscoll couldn't wait to get started in a morning,' posed Stony Crags with a guttural chortle.

Garrison skewered him with a brutal grimace. This was no time for facetious comments.

'If'n you ain't got nothing useful to contribute,' he shot back acidly, 'Then keep that big trap booted.'

Cragg's ugly features reddened. Low sniggers from behind made his hackles rise at the put-down. But he grudgingly accepted the advice.

'Only one way to find out,' said Quail, removing a Henry rifle from its scabbard and checking the load.

The gang boss nodded.

'Keep your eyes peeled,' he warned the others leading the way down a shallow gradient. 'That gal could be waiting to ambush us.'

Tentatively, the group of riders approached the seemingly deserted camp. It was a hard-boiled gunslick, who went by the name of the Arkansas Kid, who drew Garrison's attention to the occupant of the large hole.

'Take a peek down here, boss,' he hallooed. Hands on hips, he couldn't resist a hearty chuckle of derision at the unfortunate plight of the prisoner.

Coonskin Lamaar had been asleep. It was the Kid's strident yell to his confederates that brought him abruptly awake. Garrison hurried across and peered into the dark pit. The others crowded round the edge. What the gang boss perceived brought a louring growl to his pursed lips. His pockmarked nose twitched.

Drawing his pistol, he aimed it at the cowering weasel. Lamaar backed away in abject terror, eyes bulging as he stared down the barrel.

'What did I tell you about failing me again?'

The revolver's hammer clicked back, ominously loud in the stillness of the afternoon. The little fellow was a whisker away from meeting the grim reaper when he found his voice.

'Don't shoot, boss.' The choked words echoed round the dank walls of his tomb.

'Give me one good reason why I shouldn't?'

'Just hear me out,' he implored. 'I can lead you to the whereabouts of a hidden stash that'll make this claim seem like chicken feed.'

Garrison's trigger finger eased back slightly. Anger and frustration with this sorry excuse for a man was tempered by the possibility of easy loot for the taking. Quickly the business side of his character took over.

'Why should I believe you?' he rapped, shaking the gun at the quaking weasel. 'A skunk facing a bullet in the brain will say anything to save his miserable hide.'

'Its true! Cross my heart!' pleaded Lamaar. 'Over the border in Bronco Canyon west of Stovepipe Wells there's a hoard of gold nuggets just waiting to be picked up. And I should know, cos I hid 'em there.'

Garrison continued to hold him with a sceptical leer. But the pistol was no longer pointing at Lamaar's head. For what seemed like a lifetime, the gang boss hovered above the quaking captive, a lethal predator playing with its victim.

Then he signalled to Randy Quail.

'Get that pesky weasel out of there.' And to the Arkansas Kid, 'Have a forage around the camp. See if you can dig out the makings of a pot of coffee and some grub. This guy has a tale to tell.' He pulled out a cigar, bit off the end, and lit up. 'And it better be convincing. Cos if it ain't. . . .'

A frigid chortle, cold as a boot hill corpse, left Coonskin in no doubt as to what his fate would be.

Garrison moved away as Randy Quail manoeuvered a ladder down into the hole.

TEN

BETRAYED

Coonskin Lamaar had been down on his luck when he first came into contact with his future partner. Along with a heap of similar derelicts who were experiencing a blip in their fortunes, he was splayed out on a straw mattress in a flophouse dormitory in the Arizona border town of Palo Verde.

Most of the beds were similarly occupied by men who didn't even have the wherewithal for a beer in the local saloon, let alone a comfortable bed in a hotel. And it showed. Bare walls stained a dirty yellow by innumerable stogies gave the place an air of despondency. A smoky tallow lamp was the only source of illumination. And over all hung the rank odour of unwashed bodies, stale beer and failure in abundance.

Stuck on the edge of town, it was as if the local council had tried to keep it out of sight. This was not the sort of establishment that a thriving town wanted to advertise.

'Next time I find me a good source of paydirt,' grumbled Lamaar to anyone willing to listen, 'I'll make damned certain my partners is honest and reliable. And not swindlers waiting to fleece a guy when he ain't looking.'

Lamaar had been ranting on for the last half-hour. Complaining of how he had made and lost two fortunes in gold, both to unscrupulous n'er-do-wells, it was a tale of woe often played out in the shabby dormitory.

Most of the other occupants had heard it all before. A rhythmic snoring ought to have informed the speaker that he had gone on long enough. His diatribe had long since bored them into a deep sleep. Lamaar was too obtuse for that.

But one resident was wide awake. Splayed out on the adjacent cot, a bewhiskered guy in his early fifties had been listening, carefully absorbing every word.

Casually he piped up, 'How did you lose your pokes, then?'

Always keen to encourage an audience Lamaar sat up and faced his neighbour. A tall dude whom he judged to be around six four lay with his head resting on folded arms. Worn boots overhung the end of the cot by a good six inches. Eyes of deepest brown stared back at Lamaar. They were ensconced within a heavily lined face. Experience and hardship were stamped all over the ribbed contours in equal measure. And every crease appeared to have a story to unfold.

Lamaar immediately sensed a kindred spirit.

'The name is Jeb Stockwell,' announced his new buddy. 'I came out here to maybe raise some cattle. But road agents robbed me of everything I had. Left me flat broke. That's how come I ended up in a dump like this.' A lazy arm idly encompassed the bleak surroundings.

The man's deep tones suggested he hailed from back East, Kentucky maybe. Lamaar accepted the proffered hand. The shake was firm, that of a man who knew his way around. Although perhaps a mite green around the gills, judging by his recent admission.

'Coonskin Lamaar,' came back the reply. Then he proceeded to answer the guy's query. 'Same as you in a way. My first partner stole three months' worth of hard graft during the night. Just upped sticks and left while I was asleep. Never did find the varmint. That was five years back.'

'And the other?'

'Two bandits robbed me as I was heading for the assay office at Prescott.' Lamaar's mouth broke into a lurid smile. 'Took me a while, but I tracked 'em down to Flagstaff. They won't be robbing no other prospectors, that's for darned sure.' He didn't elaborate. The meaning was clear as a church bell.

After that revelation the two men lay down, once again cocooned in their own twilight world of day-dreams.

It was Stockwell who broke the silence.

'Maybe we could do business,' the big man suggested, standing up. His loose-limbed body was that of a much younger man. Unlike Coonskin Lamaar who had always been on the thin and wiry side, Stockwell was big-boned.

He motioned for the small man to join him outside. There was little chance of any privacy in the dormitory. And what Jeb Stockwell had to propose was not for the ears of the over-curious.

Once outside they moved away from the thin walls of the flophouse. Stockwell lit up a corncob and puffed away for a few minutes before outlining his proposal.

'I need me a trustworthy partner,' he began.

Lamaar's ears were flapping like a banner in the wind.

'Yeah?'

'I've come into some information that concerns a goldfield that nobody's heard about.' Stockwell chewed hard on the pipe stem. 'I ain't no miner so I need someone to come in with me who has the knowledge to get the stuff out of the ground.'

'So where is this new bonanza?' enquired Lamaar, trying unsuccussfully to conceal his eagerness.

'Bronco Canyon on the Natanes Plateau.'

The little man sucked in his breath.

'Man, that's one bad place. Hotter than a whore's fanny on payday.' He shook his head, a sceptical frown knotting his weathered features. 'A guy would have to be real sure there was plenty of paydirt for the taking bafore he ventured into that mad ass cauldron.'

'I'm sure.' Stockwell laid blunt stress on his contention.

'How come?'

Slowly, the older man extracted a small leather pouch from his inside pocket. Reaching inside he lifted out the largest gold nugget that Lamaar had ever seen.

The little man gasped. His mouth hung agape. Ogling peepers bulged wide in the presence of such magnificence. The late afternoon sun caught the knobbly edges, making the nugget wink and sparkle, perfectly displaying the hypnotic allure that pure gold always possesses. Gingerly, reverently almost, the little man took hold of the heavy object, stroking and caressing it with deferential admiration.

An avaricious glint of fire sparkled in his fervid gaze. His mouth formed words of awe, but nothing emerged. Such was the mesmeric effect of the nugget.

'Where in tarnation did you get a hold of this little beauty?' he babbled, eventually relocating his voice.

'An old Apache gave it to me for saving his hide. He'd slipped down a ravine and broken his leg. Would have died for sure if'n I hadn't come along. I fished him out and set it straight, then delivered him back to the tribe. They were wintering in the lee of the Coronado Mountains. Turned out the old boy was a chief. When I questioned him,' Stockwell paused, nodding at the glittering object, 'it turned out he'd just picked it up while passing through Badwater Basin on the Natanes.'

Lamaar whistled.

'So you want a partner to help locate the rest?'

Stockwell nodded.

'What's the deal then?'

'Fifty-fifty. Equal partners, straight down the middle.' Stockwell held out a hand. 'Agreed?'

'You betcha!' exclaimed Lamaar without any hesitation. He grabbed the extended paw to seal the bargain. The thought of discovering a heap of similar-sized baubles had effectively dispelled any misgivings about the Natanes Plateau that Coonskin Lamaar might have entertained.

'And this little fella will finance the operation,' added Stockwell.

A couple of days later, the two intrepid gold-seekers were on the trail heading east. They were accompanied by a recalcitrant *burro* named Buckweed who was loaded down with enough supplies for a month. Their destination: Badwater Basin, one of the hottest points on the continent. After savouring the sublime euphoria occasioned by the nature of the expedition, the pragmatic difficulties associated with their task were rapidly sinking in.

Lack of water would be their main problem. Not only for mere survival. A regular supply was essential for sifting the ore-bearing gravel beds.

It was three weeks later that the small party descended a long gentle gradient which brought them on to the broad flatlands where gold nuggets by the bucketful were supposedly just waiting to be scooped up.

Badwater Basin lay in the heartland of the most desolate piece of real estate in America.

The following days found the pair criss-crossing

the level basin in blistering temperatures. It was gruelling work with no vestige of shade to alleviate the incessant heat.

But of the yellow hoard, there was no sign.

And their water bottles were almost empty. Although there was a source of water on the flats, it was saline and only served to increase their thirst.

Tempers were beginning to fray.

'You sure that old goat wasn't playing you for a sucker, Jeb?' scowled Coonskin Lamaar with a harsh sneer. 'There ain't nothing in this God-forsaken hell hole but mesquite and salt.'

Stockwell himself was beginning to wonder.

'Maybe we ought to cut across to the far rim and investigate the canyonlands,' he suggested.

'Can't be worse than this,' concurred Lamaar.

So it was agreed. They pointed their mounts west towards the distant Pinaleño Range. Buckweed snorted, equally keen to vacate the searing wilderness of Badwater Basin.

The discovery of paydirt was proving far more elusive than either of the prospectors had envisioned. They could only hope and pray that Lady Luck would turn up trumps in Bronco Canyon. The trek across the endless stretch composed of white salt pans took three days.

When they eventually reached the foothills on the far side, at least there was a regular water supply available, if only a trickle.

But after a week of searching they had found nothing. Once again the old Apache seemed to be laughing at them.

But Jeb Stockwell was convinced they were in the right area.

'It has to be round here some place,' he pressed without pausing in the endless sifting of gravel. 'I can just feel it in my bones.'

Lamaar grunted. He was not so gullible. Half-heartedly, he searched the riffle box for any signs of the golden gleam. Nothing, as usual. In fact, he was becoming disenchanted with the whole caper.

The following night over the usual supper of refried beans and tortillas, he voiced his discontent.

'If we ain't found anything by sundown tomorrow,' he stated emphatically, 'I'm pulling out.'

Stockwell was not surprised.

'Where you figure on heading?' he enquired.

Lamaar shrugged. 'Back to the western slopes of the Sierra Nevada. It may be crowded with miners over there, but at least we know they've struck gold all along the valley.'

Stockwell considered for a moment. His forehead puckered in thought.

'How about giving it another two days,' he said at last. 'If we ain't struck paydirt by then, I'll come with you.' Peering over the flickering embers of the fire, he held the younger man's challenging regard. 'What d'you say?'

Smoke from Lamaar's cigar twirled in the static air.

'Not a minute longer!'

It was mid-afternoon on the last day.

Stockwell had decided to investigate the far end of the canyon. Intermittent clusters of pickleweed, horsetail and greasewood provided some relief from the barren landscape of broken rock surging up on either flank. The prospector had actually come to value the harsh rigor of its emptiness. Unlike many prospectors, he actually enjoyed the solitude. But unless they could uncover the gold that he felt certain was here, then Bronco Canyon held no future. He screwed his eyes against the harsh sunlight, idly scanning the bleak wilderness.

He dismounted, sat on a rock and dug out his pipe. So this was it. All the hard work for nothing. A black-tailed jackrabbit leapt on to a nearby rock. It rose on to its hind legs. To Stockwell's peeved mind, the creature appeared to be mocking him.

Frustration finally boiled over.

'What in thunder are you clucking at?' he hollered.

The animal just sat there smirking.

Stockwell picked up a stone to throw. He hefted it. Then suddenly he realized it was far heavier than any normal rock. He gave it a closer inspection. Staring back at him were streaks of yellow embedded in the rough stone. Hardly daring to think he had found the tantalizing prize, he feverishly searched the immediate surroundings. Was it just a maverick, a one-off?

Then he saw another, two more over there.

This was it!

Apache gold.

All on his ownsome, except for a thoroughly bemused jackrabbit, Jeb Stockwell danced a merry jig, howling with glee as he did so.

The two partners moved their camp to the head of the canyon. Within a week they had amassed as much gold as they could carry. There was plenty more left over for which they could return once the claim had been legally registered.

The nearest trail crossing the Natanes Plateau was at Stovepipe Wells. They would have to cross the notorious sand dunes to reach the trading post.

And that was what proved their downfall.

Lack of water and the soft sand were too much for even a tough *burro* to handle indefinitely. Especially one overladen with the yellow stuff. Buckweed keeled over before they had even started across the sands. And there was no way that the horses could absorb the extra load.

'We're gonna have to hide the goods around here someplace and come back when we've bought a couple of new *burros*,' commented Lamaar.

His partner agreed. They quickly unloaded the sacks and interred them in a small cave in the shadow of a prominent crag, erecting a marker cairn for identification.

'Nobody'll find the stuff in there,' commented Stockwell, eyeing his partner's skinny frame.

'Good thing you took me on as yer partner then, ain't it?' returned Lamaar, baring his yellowed teeth in what passed for a smile. Then he continued, 'Anyway, let's be getting out of here. We don't have time to waste jawing.'

Lamaar mounted up and led the way across the endless sandy ocean.

Having safely crossed the dunes, they found a trail

winding up a rough slope to crest a gap in the mountains known as Gunsight Pass. Thereafter, the route narrowed as it descended to the trading post at Stovepipe Wells.

Lamaar reined up.

'It's getting late,' he remarked, offering the suggestion that they camp there for the night. An early start would see them at the Wells before noon the following day where they could secure the much-needed *burros*. Stockwell had no objections.

All through the meal Lamaar was unusually quiet, preoccupied.

Stockwell assumed his partner was thinking about the return for the gold.

Suddenly the little guy stood up and wandered over to the edge of the pass where it plunged down into a deep ravine. For five minutes he remained there, just staring into the void.

'Something bothering you, Coonskin?' Stockwell lumbered to his feet, a puzzled frown lacing his contours. 'You don't seem your usual self today,' he said, approaching Lamaar from behind.

Then it happened. There was no warning.

In a single fluid movement, the little man swung on his heel and drove a lethal Bowie knife into the exposed guts of his partner. Stockwell was taken completely by surprise. He staggered back, right hand clutching at the deadly blade embedded in his stomach.

Their eyes met. And in that instant, Stockwell took heed of the avaricious leer on his partner's face, the piggy eyes pulsating with pure greed. He could now see the leech that had been eating away at Lamaar's guts ever since the critter had first set eyes on that lone nugget of gold back at Palo Verde. So this had been his intention all along. To rob his partner and take all the loot for himself.

Lamaar's ugly puss twisted into a loathsome grimace as he came forward to finish the job.

'You thieving varmint!' croaked Stockwell as blood dribbled from his mouth. With a final supreme effort born out sheer determination to avenge his betrayal, the dying man drew his revolver. 'If I can't have my share of the goods, then neither will you.'

The rapacious gloating on Lamaar's face was instantly replaced by one of fear. But he was a slippery weasel, quick on the uptake. He lunged at the injured man, snatching his own sidearm from its holster.

Two shots blasted the silence of Gunsight Pass. And each found its mark.

Stockwell cried out as a heavy slug punched into his shoulder. His own bullet had creased the traitor's head, souring his aim.

Momentarily, silence once again engulfed the lonely campsite before a third shot rang out. The resonant echo bounced off the rock walls enclosing the pass. The double-dealing rat lurched backwards. He teetered on the edge of the ravine, arms frantically clutching at the air. Through the agonizing gaze that clouded Stockwell's vision, he appeared to be watching a dance of death.

A howl of anguish at his thwarted endeavour erupted from between Lamaar's quivering lips. Then he tumbled headlong into the grasping embrace of the deep cutting. The abhorrent Judas had made his final curtain call.

Or so Jeb Stockwell assumed.

ELEVEN

DEAD MAN WALKING

'So what d'yuh reckon, boss?'

'A load of eyewash if'n you ask me,' barked Randy Quail. 'I say we gun him down and bury the sneaky rat in that hole.'

Garrison ignored the interjection.

Following Lamaar's revelation about the hidden stash of gold, Diamond Jim had stood up and was pacing around the camp. There was a lot to think about. How much of the guy's story was true? There again, did it really matter if he had embellished it to suit his own ends? Just so long as the gold was where he said it was.

And there was only one way to find out.

Garrison stopped in front of the quaking prospector. His hand rested on the butt of his revolver. A finger tapped idly. It sounded like the metronome of death. But Garrison's icy glare, blank and impenetrable, gave nothing away.

Lamaar sensed that a decision had been made. He couldn't help wondering if Randy Quail's grim smirk would be rewarded.

'If you kill me,' he said nervously but with a pointed emphasis, 'then nobody gets the gold. I'm the only person alive who knows where it's hidden.'

'You gotten a map then?' There was an underhanded twist to the Arkansas Kid's apparently innocent enquiry.

Lamaar tapped his head. 'All up here.' He couldn't resist a wry chuckle. 'Safer than a bank vault.'

'What about that partner of your'n?' enquired the cynical Randy Quail, 'This Jeb Stockwell. He could have dug the gold up by now.'

This was something nobody else had considered.

They turned as one back to Lamaar. Hostility reflected from staring eyes that glowed red in the flickering light cast by the fire.

'Not a chance!' scoffed Lamaar. The suggestion elicited a brittle laugh. 'The guy was skewered good. A ten-inch Bowie saw to that. And I managed to put a bullet in him for good measure. When I went over the edge of that ravine, he was leaking like a sieve. Even if he'd managed to survive the night, the poor sap would have bled to death afore he could reach help.' He peered around at the hard faces. 'No!' he stressed, 'I'm the only one who can lead you to the gold.'

'OK,' Garrison declared. 'We'll do it your way. But if you're playing for time, and this is some kind of trick to save your mangy hide, I'm sure that Randy here will figure out an appropriate punishment.'

The hardcase responded with a malignant chuckle. 'Be my pleasure.'

'As God is my witness,' pleaded Lamaar, crossing himself. The stress was getting to him. 'What I've told you is the honest truth.'

Garrison's response was a sceptical muttering. But nonetheless, he accepted the veracity of the little toad's account.

Lamaar breathed deep to calm his nerves. Once they had located that marker cairn near Bronco Canyon, he promised himself to quit this bunch of no-hopers and head back to excavate the real bonanza. This time on his ownsome. No more partners for Coonskin Lamaar.

'One thing has been bothering me, though,' Garrison mused butting in on the little guy's ruminations. 'How come you were able to get out of that hell hole alive?'

'It was a slice of pure luck.' The weasel's slit of a mouth turned up at the recollection. 'I've often wondered about it myself.'

After he had disappeared over the rim into Gunsight Canyon, Lamaar was sure that his end had arrived. He bounced down a steeply canting chute of loose gravel. At the bottom, his battered frame was launched into thin air.

'They say that a man's life passes before his eyes when he's facing the grim reaper.' Lamaar shook his head. 'Believe me, boys, when I tell you it ain't so.' The gang were now hanging on to his every word

'There's no time for any of that kind of boloney. Your mind just goes completely blank.'

Next thing he was crashing through the upper canopy of trees lining the creek that flowed in the bottom of the gorge. This was what saved his bacon. It broke his headlong plummet to certain death. Eventually he came to a jarring though welcome rest in the fork of a cottonwood. From there, he was able to clamber gingerly down to ground level some ten feet below.

Shock and feverish exhaustion quickly set in. Lamaar's whole being had taken a rough scrambling. It included a broken arm that he set as best he could with a couple of solid boughs.

'Don't know how long I was unconscious.' He accepted a slug of whiskey from Arkansas and slung it down in a single belt. The reliving of his nightmare return to civilization was taking its toll. 'Could have been hours, days even. All I know is that I awoke early one morning, stiff and aching all over. But at least I was alive, and the bleeding had stopped.'

There was no way that he could climb out of the ravine, especially with that arm. Sheer walls of rock hemmed him in. Thankfully, the compressed nature of the steep-sided cut had kept the brutal power of the sun at bay.

All he could do was make his way downstream and hope that it led him back to some form of civilization where he could get medical help.

And so it had proved.

Gunsight Creek took a westerly course away from his original destination of Stovepipe Wells.

'I followed that ravine for three weeks.' Lamaar's eyes were red-rimmed and glassy as he stared into the fire. 'Survived on fish and berries. I'd almost given up hope when I stumbled on to a trading post at Paramount Springs.'

Not that he would have conceded the notion, but Garrison had been as enthralled by the recital of the rascally prospector as his men. But it now occurred to him that time might well be of the essence.

'How long is it since you stashed this gold?' he snapped brusquely.

'I figure about eight months ago.'

'And you kept it a secret all this time?' The comment was low and scathing in its frosty delivery. 'Didn't even think to share this good fortune with your buddies?'

Lamaar saw the flesh tighten around Garrison's mouth, the hand reaching for the hidden Springfield.

'I have now, ain't I?' he whined, puffing hard on a stogie. 'I was near to dying out there, and needed a spell to recover. So I hitched a ride on the first wagon heading east for Santa Fe.' Then, with a touch of bravado he asserted: 'And remember it's yours truly who knows the exact location of the gold. Kill me and you come away empty handed.' He tried to ease the tension around the fire with a nervous laugh. 'Anyways, there's enough gold out there to set us all up for life.'

Garrison relaxed. He knew that Lamaar could always be disposed of later once the loot was in his hands.

117

'Then it seems to me that we ain't got no time to waste on idle chatter.' Rising to his feet was the signal for the others to follow suit. He went across to his mount. 'I want us on the road by first light.'

As the dawning of the new day strengthened, Emma Driscoll was able to pick up the pace and make better progress along the lower valley. At first she had avoided the main trail, keeping above the creek bottom. She had no wish to encounter any other miners. Not that they would have accosted her, but if Garrison started questioning them, Emma preferred that they remain ignorant of her movements.

Once Happy Dan had been left behind, she dropped down to valley level and easier terrain.

To the west of Mogollon the trail was barely discernible. But all she was concerned with at that moment was to put as much distance between herself and the Garrison gang as possible.

Frequently she drew rein and scanned her back trail. Anxiety furrowed her brow at the thought of them catching up. As the day wore on, with no sign of any pursuit, she was able to breathe more easily. By late afternoon, she was well into the foothills of the Hidalgos. An intermittent track pursued a tortuous course between a chaotic splurge of sturdy boulders climbing ever higher into the mountain fastness. Progress was now confined to a steady plod as the gradient noticeably steepened.

Emma drew the bay mare to a halt, uncorked the metal water bottle and tipped the contents to her lips.

*

Not for the first time, Nelson paused and cast a wary eye over the way they had come. He could clearly see the course they had been following up the right side of a broad trench devoid of vegetation save for isolated clumps of beavertail cactus and Apache plume, not forgetting the ubiquitous sagebrush. They had left the dense stands of black-barked piñon behind in the lower reaches of the valley.

He took off his hat to more easily shade out the lowering sun that was dipping towards the western horizon. Narrowed eyes swept the landscape, searching. But for what?

'Something bothering you, Nelson?' asked Mick Riley. 'That's the third time in the last hour that you've had us stop.' The Irishman turned and surveyed the way they had come. 'I can't see nothing back there.'

'I get an itch in the back of my neck whenever something ain't quite as it should be,' Nelson replied, continuing to study every detail of the terrain. 'And I'm ready for a good scratch right now.'

'Man with sixth sense like bird in sky,' added Chen Shing sagely. 'Sees things ordinary mortals miss.'

'And there it is!' exclaimed Nelson, excitedly jabbing a finger. 'I knew I was right.'

'What are we looking for?' urged Riley. 'Cos I ain't no feathered flyer.'

'There it is again.'

Only for an instant, a glint of metal was reflected by the sun's light. This time, both Riley and the

Chinaman caught the brief twinkle.

'What do you reckon it could be?' asked Riley straining his peepers for a glimpse of the strange phenomenon.

'Gotta be a who, I'd say,' stressed Nelson.

'Then it has to be that asshole, Garrison,' snarled Riley clenching his fists. 'The rat musta gotten wind of our plans and has given chase.'

'I not think so,' interjected Chen.

'Why not?'

'Garrison would have gang to back him up. Him more yellow than Chinese.' The little man grimaced, then spat in the dust. 'Never go anywhere alone.'

'Chop Suey's right.' Nelson added his support to the conjecture. 'Far as I can make out, there's only one rider on the trail.'

Riley dismounted and slid a rifle out of its scabbard.

'Then we best lie up and grab him,' he said. 'See what game he's playing.'

The others had no objection and quickly joined him. They secreted the horses behind some bushes, then slid behind a conglomeration of boulders to await their mysterious trail hound.

It was another half-hour before Riley's impatience was rewarded. The clinking of shod hoofs on rock announced the imminent arrival of their shadow. A flat plainsman hat appeared over the rim of the level stretch of ground the three partners had chosen for their ambush site.

The rider's face was cloaked in shade. Nelson quickly perceived that he was alone. He allowed a gentle sigh of relief to escape through tightly clenched teeth. Nonetheless, he allowed the rider to draw nearer before stepping out from cover. A rifle was aimed at their unwanted company.

To his left stood the little Chinaman, pistol in hand.

'Haul up, mister!' snapped Nelson. The blunt command was bolstered by the wagging firearm. 'And don't try to make a run for it neither. We got your back trail covered.'

The ominous ratcheting of Riley's thumbed rifle hammer behind the rider lent added confirmation that resistance was useless. 'So you be a sensible fella.' The Emerald Isle cadence in Riley's voice concealed a blunt reminder of what the consequences of a refusal would be. 'And do like the man says, then set your pistol down.'

The rider's bowed head had been bent low as he concentrated on the trail immediately ahead. He had no inkling that a trap had been set. The sudden interruption to his thoughts jerked the rider's head back sending the hat flying and allowing the long hair beneath to escape.

It fluttered effortlessly in the breeze, revealing a startled though no less comely face. And it was one that Riley instantly recognized.

He spluttered incomprehensibly.

The other two ambushers were likewise taken aback by the pretty sight. Even Chen Shing appeared nonplussed. Riley was the first to pull himself together.

'W-what in the n-name of Saint Patrick are you

doing up here, Miss Driscoll?' he stammered.

'You acquainted with this lady?' enquired a bemused Nelson.

Riley smiled, knowing that the supposed danger was past. 'We kinda bumped into one another in Mogollon,' he said with a wry smile.

'And that's the literal truth,' added the young woman.

'This, my dear partners, is Miss Emma Driscoll,' announced the bluff Irishman. Stepping forward, he gallantly assisted the woman to the ground. Then quickly retrieved the discarded hat and handed it back to her with a flourish. A beaming grin was pasted to his ogling kisser as he continued. 'Her father had gone missing and I suggested he could be in one the saloons.' Then addressing the woman he asked, 'Did he turn up, then?'

Though innocently delivered, the question brought all the traumas of the last few days flooding back with a vengeance. Emma burst into tears. Shaken to the core, Riley was transfixed, stunned into silence by this unexpected change in circumstances.

It was left to Chen Shing to hurry forward and lead the distraught woman over to a rock, where he sat her down. A few sips of water from a canteen dispelled the ashen pallor, bringing some colour back to her smooth cheeks.

Nobody spoke.

There was clearly a story to be told here. But it was left to the disquieted woman to satisfy their curiosity in her own good time.

As it was getting late in the day, Nelson decided to make camp for the night. Following a makeshift meal, they sat round the flickering embers of the fire and considered the implications of Emma's disclosures.

The grim tale left a sickly taste in Riley's mouth.

'That man has a lot to be answering for,' he spat out. 'Next time we come across the shifty varmint, I'll skin him alive and feed him to the coyotes.'

Nelson was in full agreement. But the arrival of the woman had posed a dilemma of its own.

Excusing himself, he wandered away into the comforting embrace of the darkness. There was much to think on. He recalled with an ironic smile the story of the Ten Little Indians. Except in this case, his number of partners was increasing rather than the opposite. And therein lay the problem.

Under the circumstances, there was no possibility of sending her back down the trail into the clutches of Diamond Jim Garrison and his unsavoury gang. Whether he liked it or not, he was stuck with Emma Driscoll, at least until they reached a relay station where she could catch a ride.

Then again, he surmised, she might not want to leave their company once she learned of the hidden gold cache. According to his Uncle Jeb's map, it would be another three weeks before they reached Bronco Canyon. And during that time there would be little hope of keeping their destination a secret.

Not that he resented this sudden addition to their number. Emma was certainly no ugly duckling. A dreamy cast softened the stern expression of a moment previously. Indeed she was a heap better to look on than those two unsightly bozos with whom he was currently saddled. And that was clad in rough working garb. In a fine dress with her Titian hair coiffured. . . .

Nelson would not have been so relaxed had he been aware of a similarly amorous regard with which Mick Riley was viewing their new recruit across the dancing flames of the campfire.

TWELVE

STOVEPIPE WELLS

'What did I tell yuh?'

Coonskin Lamaar was almost jumping for joy in the saddle. He jabbed a finger at the trading post that had suddenly hove into view. The group of riders had just crested a low rise. And there it was, on the edge of a rolling ocean of sand that stretched away into the distance.

Stovepipe Wells Trading Post.

'This better not be a wild-goose chase you've brought us on,' barked the glowering gang boss.

After three weeks' continuous riding, Garrison's natty suit was stained and caked in trail dust. The jaunty brown derby was dented and sweat-stained. Never a patient man, his temper had become increasingly fractious over the last few days. He'd been snapping at the slightest excuse, and even Randy Quail was more than relieved to sight the welcoming settlement.

'All we have to do now is get to the far side of the dunes.' Lamaar shrugged off Garrison's implied threat to his air supply. 'Then we'll all be in clover.'

'How long will that take?' from, Stony Cragg.

'No more'n a week,' replied Lamaar. 'Providing we don't rush things.'

This was not what Garrison wanted to hear. He snorted impatiently, but did not put his frustration into words until some time later.

Lamaar knew that for the time being it was all bluster. Garrison's threats were toothless. The guy needed Lamaar to locate the gold. Until then, the little weasel knew that he was safe.

His next remark laid particular emphasis on caution. 'Crossing the dunes is the hardest bit. We'll need to rest up and take on extra water. There ain't hardly enough to fill a thimble out there.' A lazily waving arm panned the empty wilderness they would have to traverse. 'I found that out the hard way, remember.'

The old prospector spurred his faded mount down the gentle slope towards the distant cluster of buildings that represented the only source of water in this part of the Natanes Plateau.

The others followed behind. They were all keen to avail themselves of whatever primitive facilities the trading post had to offer.

As they neared the Wells the Arkansas Kid piped up: 'How did this dive get its name, Coonskin?' There was more than a hint of respect in the way he asked the question.

Lamaar was in a buoyant mood, relishing his unexpected though agreeable status. However short-lived it might be.

'This part of the valley is subject to a lot of drifting sand,' Lamaar explained. He was now in his element. 'The water supply would have been filled in if some bright spark hadn't seen fit to mark its location with a stovepipe.' His eyes suddenly lit up. 'And there it is!'

Four pairs of curious eyes followed his pointing finger. A three-foot hunk of rusting iron pipe was sticking out of the ground to one side of the trading post.

'It ain't much,' scoffed Randy Quail.

'That well is a life-saver out here,' stressed the cocky weasel, injecting an authoritative edge to his voice. 'Just remember that.'

The man in black seethed at the put-down, but kept silent. He could wait.

After tying off their tired mounts to the hitching rail, the five men entered the dim interior and bellied up to a rough-hewn plank bar supported by two empty beer barrels.

'What'll it be then, gents?' enquired the grubby proprietor who went by the unlikely monicker of Soapy Scott.

'Beers all round,' replied Garrison. He removed his hat and wiped a once-white handkerchief across his salt-encrusted brow.

'And keep 'em coming,' added Quail.

The hard-boiled jasper twisted round, idly resting his elbows on the bar top. Sporting an arrogant sneer, he surveyed the spartan surroundings. That was when he noticed they were not alone.

Over in a corner, three Indians sat hunched around a bottle of rot-gut. Through the gloomy mist that hung over the interior, Quail could see they were no threat. One was old with a bronzed face, weathered and wrinkled like a dried plum. His companions were younger, no more than kids.

'You serve any piece of dog trash in this dump?'

Quail's offensive enquiry, though addressed to the proprietor, was spoken sufficiently loudly for the Indians to hear. Whether they understood mattered little to the gunslinger. Only a slight lift of the shoulders from the oldest of them indicated that the insulting jibe had not gone unnoticed. But that was all.

'A man has to take what business he can in a backwater like Stovepipe Wells,' shrugged Soapy, anxious to avoid any trouble. Shifty eyes flickered across to the Apaches. 'This place might have the only water supply within fifty miles, but it don't mean I'm overloaded with customers.' Then, as an afterthought, he added, 'And they pay in gold. That's all I'm bothered about.'

'Gold, yuh say?' A wild look had come over the twitchy visage of Coonskin Lamaar.

'The genuine stuff.' A fiery gleam flared in the trader's beady peepers. 'You fellers after doing some prospecting?'

'Just passing through,' asserted Garrison, rather too briskly.

Unwittingly, it was Stony Cragg who averted any awkward questions.

'Man, in high summer this place must be like Hell itself,' he gasped. 'Even now, it's hot enough to melt the eyes of a jackrabbit.' Cragg was suffering from the incessant heat more than the others on account of the excessive bulk he was forced to haul around.

Scott accepted the bait.

'This is cool compared to what it's like over on the sand dunes,' the trader assured them as he tapped out the beers. 'I warned them other travellers about it. But would they listen? No sirree! Thought they knew better than ol' Soapy. Well, I can tell you fellas, they'll soon wish they'd taken my advice. Nobody can survive out there for long. Excepting the Indians, of course.'

Garrison's sagging frame suddenly stiffened. Other riders crossing the sands? Who could they be? Surely no one else could be heading for Bronco Canyon. He brusquely quashed Soapy Scott's flow of information with a curt interjection.

'When was this?'

'Two days ago.'

'How many of them was there?'

The trader eyed the gang leader warily. A tightness around the jawline matched the louring frown. He peered at each of the hard faces in turn before answering.

'Four riders . . . and one was a funny little dwarf. Chinese if I ain't mistaken.'

The gang leader gulped. He couldn't disguise the shocked expression that stood out on his face.

Chen Shing!

It had to be him. The odds of there being two such

129

dwarfs in Arizona at this particular time were too high for it to be a coincidence. So what was he doing here? And who were his sidekicks?

Bulging eyes and an open mouth suggested to Soapy Scott that these were no ordinary travellers crossing the Natanes. His gaze narrowed. Maybe he could turn this situation to his advantage.

Ostentatiously scratching at his ear, he tried to affect a casual nonchalance. 'One of them was a girl. Mighty handsome as well, even under them working duds.'

'That has to be the Driscoll dame,' blurted Randy Quail. 'Somehow she must have teamed up with—'

'Shut up!' rapped Garrison. Shocked astonishment upon learning of this new development had quickly been thrust aside. It was replaced by a ruthless determination not to disclose any of their plans to this nosy trader. He signalled for them to move away to a far table out of earshot.

Coonskin Lamaar alone remained at the bar.

The unexpected revelation that others could be on the same trail as themselves was too much for the old reprobate. He had to know the truth.

'Say, mister?' He spoke barely above a whisper.

'Yep?'

'About eight months back. . . .' He stopped. A cold sweat erupted across his forehead. Shakily, he took a gulp of his drink to calm his pounding heart. But deep down, within his very soul, he knew the answer to his proposed enquiry.

'Well?' repeated Scott leaning forward eagerly.

'Did an old dude come this way by the name of . . .

Jeb Stockwell?' The name emerged as little more than a dusty croak.

'You and this jigger acquainted, then?'

Lamaar remained tight-lipped.

'Now let me think.' Scott was milking this situation for all it was worth. 'Jeb Stockwell, you say. . . . As I recall, there was such a gent of that name brought in here. Two army scouts found him. In a bad way he was. Near on died in my arms from that knife wound.' Scott shook his greasy head with an exagerated measure of mock concern.

'What happened to him?'

'It was lucky for him the army patrol called in here two days later with a medic in tow,' replied Scott. 'They patched him up, then continued west. Last I heard he'd ended up in a hospital in Flagstaff.'

Garrison had immediately cottoned on to Lamaar's intentions when the old guy remained at the bar. He was standing at his shoulder when this information was received.

'Was Stockwell with this bunch who went over the dunes?' he snapped out.

By this time Soapy Scott knew he was on to a good thing. He picked up a glass and briskly polished it, dragging out the silence.

'Seems like all this information I'm passing over could be worth more than just the price of a few drinks,' he suggested with a meaningful leer creasing his ugly puss. 'What d'yuh say then, boys? Seems like we're all in business . . . of one sort or another.' A grubby open paw was held out expectantly.

'Why, you no-good chiseller,' spat Randy Quail,

reaching for his pistol.

'Easy now, Randy,' chided Diamond Jim, staying his bodyguard's hand. 'Mr Scott here has a legitimate point. He's given us some valuable information. And that deserves to be rewarded.' He extracted a thick billfold from his suit pocket and peeled off $200.

Scott's eyes bulged. He hadn't ever seen that much dough in one place before. But the green-eyed monster was hard at work.

'Seems like the griff I've passed over is worth a heap more'n that.'

Garrison's face was set hard in a fixed smile, icy cold in its intensity as he handed over $200 more.

'So was Stockwell with them?' he rasped acidly.

'No,' asserted Scott. 'Just a big Irish jackass and a young shaver he kept calling Nelson, as well as the other two.'

Garrison's head was spinning. He was in a dead funk.

So Nelson had survived as well.

It was almost too much to digest at one sitting. Eventually he shook the dust from his addled brain, sunk the last dregs of his beer and pushed away from the bar. Without another word, he swung on his heel and went outside into the blazing heat of late afternoon.

He hawked a gob of phlegm into the dust. Nobody uttered a word whilst they replenished their canteens and watered the horses.

This was the last news the gang boss had expected or wanted to hear – another group of gold-seekers after claiming his loot. And these were no ordinary interlopers. People he had figured were long since out his life had suddenly been resurrected.

Lamaar was tending to a cut on his cayuse's front leg. His mind was likewise focusing on other matters. It was racing nineteen to the dozen. He now realized that Jeb Stockwell, his erstwhile partner, must have died of his injuries. Otherwise he would have come back to dig up his own goods.

But what about his copy of the treasure map?

The crafty cove must have mailed it to that nephew he was always warbling on about – Horatio Muckleheimer.

That was when the truth hit him with the force of a raging tornado.

Horatio . . . Nelson. One and the same.

And they were two days in front.

Nobody spoke as the gang left the trading post.

Heading south towards the wasteland of sprawling sand dunes, it was Randy Quail who broke the tense silence that hung over them like a black cloud.

A dog was snapping at the heels of his boss's mount. Garrison was still in a daze. Quail drew his revolver and pumped a full load into the unfortunate mutt. The animal's punctured body quivered briefly, then lay still. Overhead, a pair of vultures greedily eyed the shattered corpse as the line of riders passed by. No one else gave it a glance.

But the harsh blast had seen fit to rouse Diamond Jim from his lethargic torpor.

'You shouldn't oughta have given that greedy rat

any dough, boss,' averred Quail, spurring his mount up beside that of Garrison whilst reloading the revolver. 'I could have blasted him into the middle of next week.'

The gang leader turned, offering him a crafty slant.

'And so you shall, Randy.' He smirked, slapping his sidekick on the back. Garrison had quickly regained his composure. A plan was already forming in his devious brain to thwart their adversaries. 'So you shall. That slimy dude was far too nosy for his own good. But we'll wait until we've gotten hold of the gold first. No sense in leaving dead bodies lying around for any passing drifter to come across.'

Stony Cragg gave this statement dutiful consideration, then said, 'But there was only one old jasper to get rid of. He wouldn't have given us any bother.'

Garrison regarded the hulking bruiser with piteous disdain. He lit up a cigar before making an acerbic rejoinder.

'You may not have noticed, lunkhead,' he rapped, 'but there were three redskins in there as well. One body is easy to conceal, but four would be messy. They could have given us trouble. We wouldn't want to leave any trace of our passing, now would we?'

Lamaar lent his weight to the argument by adding scornfully, 'And how do we know the rest of the tribe ain't close by?'

Garrison nodded in agreement. 'Them

Mescaleros are mean devils to get on the wrong side of.'

The lumbering tough looked suitably abashed.

'Sorry, boss.'

THIRTEEN

SNAKE EYES

Nelson gingerly sucked in a breath of the heavy dust-laden air. Its searing grittiness scoured the back of his mouth. The desire to tip a canteen of precious water down his gullet was overpowering. With a supreme effort he held back. Grit-filled eyes rimed with a hard shell of salt lifted reluctantly to survey the lie of the land.

For six days the endless carpet of pale orange had stared fiercely back at him. Only the occasional clumps of mesquite broke the dulling monotony of the dunes as the four riders trudged steadily and remorselessly onward. Silently, Nelson mouthed a prayer of thanks to the Big Guy upstairs for sparing their mounts whose heads now hung listlessly, muzzles dragging in the hot sand.

Cresting yet another of the ocean waves of sand, he suddenly reined up. Stiff muscles eased out of the saddle as he stepped down and peered into the throbbing heat haze. Everything seemed to shimmer and bubble like water lapping against a distant shore. He knuckled his tired eyes to ensure that what he had witnessed was no freak of nature, no mirage.

Another look. Yes it was still there.

Signalling for the others to join him, Nelson pointed to the crack in the wall of rock that thrust out of the barren expanse of desolation immediately ahead. For the last two days the mountains of the Paramount Range had been playing tricks with their bleary senses.

A quick check of the torn map, a curt nod of the head. This had to be their destination.

'Bronco Canyon!' The exclamation, meant to be a cry of triumph, emerged as little more than a hoarse rasp.

After seven days in the blistering heat, the sight was something of an anticlimax. All any of them wanted at this stage was a taste of the cool spring water that supposedly issued from the base of the cliff face.

Nelson coughed up a lump of sandy phlegm and spat in the dust, then repeated the announcement with more conviction.

'Well, folks, this is the end of the trail,' he announced, trying to inject the words with a breezy lilt.

'And none too soon neither,' added Mick Riley, shaking his canteen. 'We're plumb out of the wet stuff to be sure.'

'So this is what all the fuss is about?'

Emma Driscoll stood with hands on hips. She had

handled the crossing of the dunes better than any of her male companions. Perhaps it was having spent much of her young life in the company of a grizzled old prospector. She tipped the last of the water into her battered hat and offered it to her cayuse. The tired beast slurped gratefully at the life-giving sustenance.

Chen Shing had suffered the most from the hardships of the crossing. His diminutive frame had barely coped with the ravaging torment of the desert. At one stage Riley had been forced to tether the little man to his horse to prevent him tumbling out of the saddle. Another day without adequate water and shade from the brutal sun could quite easily have been his last.

Nelson offered his canteen to the Chinaman.

Chen shook his head.

'Drink!'

The snippety command brooked no rebuttal. Chen was too whacked to argue and sank the last of the water in a single swallow, nodding his thanks.

It was late morning when the four gold-seekers eventually reached the entrance to Bronco Canyon.

Surging tiers of fractured rock reared up on either side of the enormous rent in the rock wall. Huge boulders littered the canyon bottom, having broken away from the parent crag at some time in the far past.

To the right the sun beamed through a wind-scoured hole akin to the eye of a needle. A mesmeric sight. And, at the base of this strange formation, the all-important spring. Although it was found to be little more than a trickle. Even so, the presence of the life-giving substance had encouraged numerous small plants such as desert velvet and dune primrose to flourish. They lent a touch of welcome colour to the harsh landscape.

They made camp in the shade of an overhang close to the tiny spring. But such was its meagre offering that it was mid-afternoon before a single canteen had been filled. Beggars can't be choosers, however, and according to Jeb Stockwell, this was the only water within fifty miles. So they were stuck with it.

Of far more importance as far as Nelson was concerned was the pin-pointing of a rocky outcrop known as Flat Nose Butte. It was marked on the map as the key to the location of the hidden stash.

Whilst Emma tended to Chen Shing, who was suffering from heat stroke, he and Riley scoured every nook and cranny for three miles on either side of the canyon entrance trying to find the elusive landmark. But with no success.

Back at the camp, Nelson was getting ever more frustrated.

'It has to be here some place,' he railed, angrily jabbing at the offending outline that his uncle had sketched on to the map. 'Why can't we find it?'

Riley shrugged. 'Are you certain this is the right canyon?' he said.

'Of course I'm sure,' shouted Nelson irritably, shaking his fist in the air. 'It's here on the darned map. We haven't come across any other canyon breaking through the Paramounts on this side of the range, have we?'

'OK, OK,' apologized Riley, holding up his hands to placate his friend. 'I ain't the one whose made the blasted thing disappear.'

Nelson immediately regretted the uncharacteristic outburst.

'Sorry for sounding off,' he replied, somewhat crestfallen. 'I know it's not anyone's fault, excepting perhaps my uncle's.'

He rolled a quirley and inhaled the smoke allowing it to calm his frayed nerves.

By this time it was early evening. The dying sun had slipped over the threshold of the crenellated peaks. Thick shadows were slowly creeping over the landscape painting a very different picture from that evident during the harsh glare of day. And with the dying sun the rocky outlines were changing shape. Dark streaks of purple and grey enhanced the fractured rock displacements creating weird and wonderful contortions as night advanced its tentacles over the land.

It was Emma Driscoll who first noticed the phenomenon.

'Over there!' she exclaimed leaping to her feet. The spilled coffee mug went unheeded. 'Look!'

Her strident cry drew their attention to her stabbing finger.

'Flat Nose Butte.'

Both Nelson and Riley snapped out the exclamation together. Silhouetted against the yellowing backdrop of early evening, the clarity of this most welcome image was already fading. But there was no doubting the shadowy delineation – a man's head sporting that distinctive appendage.

Another three minutes and it had disappeared altogether, absorbed into the dusky opacity. But that brief appearance was sufficient for them to mark its position some 200 yards west of the canyon entrance.

'Too late for any searching now,' emoted their regalvanized leader, 'But at first light we can find out if Uncle Jeb really did strike it rich.'

'It's them all right.'

Coonskin Lamaar was splayed out on the crest of a low hill overlooking the entrance to Bronco Canyon.

Crouched down on his right side was Diamond Jim Garrison. All pretence at maintaining the sartorial elegance he normally favoured had long since been abandoned. When push came to shove, it was the acquisition of the gold that mattered. Then he could sport any number of custom-made suits.

Garrison had set a gruelling pace across the dunes. He had commandeered fresh mounts and extra water canteens to ensure the crossing was achieved in double-quick time. Even so, it had been like stepping into the jaws of hell-fire, and an experience none of them wished to repeat. Pure greed had kept them going.

For Garrison there was the added incentive of eradicating Horatio Muckleheimer once and for all. There was also the question of the girl. Whilst she was still around, he could not legitimately take control of the Happy Dan claim.

It appeared that the brutal pace had been worth while.

Thin lips drew back in a lurid grin.

Even in the fading light Garrison was able to recognize the profile of his Nemesis. And to add proof to the pudding, there was the bent, dwarfish form of Chen Shing hobbling across the clearing. He was going to enjoy watching that treacherous freak squirm before dispatching him to join his jaundiced ancestors.

Of the Irishman there was no immediate sign. But he had to be close by.

The gang boss growled, the hairs on his neck bristling with rancour.

'Doesn't look as if they've had time to dig up the lucre as yet,' he observed whilst assiduously studying the layout of the camp.

'What's the plan, Diamond Jim?'

Garrison eyed his second-in-command, a dark frown ribbing his brow. Only Randy Quail was ever allowed to be so familiar, and then only on special occasions. The gunman caught the steely glint reflected by an opalescent moon hanging low in the northern sky. He shivered involuntarily. Had he over-stepped the mark?

But Garrison let it pass.

'We wait for those poor suckers to do all the dirty work,' he smirked. 'And while they're otherwise engaged, we cut them off from the spring.' His pointing finger picked out the thin streak of silver at the base of the natural arch. 'That way we got 'em trapped like rats with no way out. They'll have to surrender the goods, or risk dying of thirst.'

'Good thinking, boss,' agreed Arkansas.

Ignoring the compliment, Garrison added with a wry chuckle: 'Only thing is, we'll make darned sure they won't be leaving Bronco Canyon tomorrow, or any other day.'

'What yuh gonna do with 'em, boss?' asked Stony Cragg.

Garrison shook his head. He angled a pitying look at the slow-witted tough. Where did he get these turkeys from? The others laughed at Cragg's naïveté.

'Keep the noise down,' hissed Garrison. 'We don't want them saps to know there's anybody else within fifty miles of here.' He indicated for the gang to retire down the back slope of the sand dune. 'And it'll be a cold supper tonight.' Heeding the youngest member of the gang, he added in a curt whisper: 'And no smoking. Got that, Arkansas?'

The Kid answered with a reluctant sigh, then nodded, slotting the sack of Bull Durham back into his vest pocket. It was going to be a long night, but the rewards would be worth it.

'Stony, you take first watch. And keep your eyes peeled. Any strange moves from the camp, I want to know. Got that?'

'Sure thing, boss,' replied Cragg, crawling back up to the lip of the dune.

The false dawn found Nelson shaking his partners awake.

Chen Shing had made a surprising recovery following a good night's rest. He quickly rekindled the dying embers of the fire and brewed a pot of coffee. Breakfast could wait.

Another half-hour and the sun had risen above the eastern horizon, lighting up the canyon wall.

Shouldering picks and shovels, Nelson and Riley hustled along the base of the rock wall to the point identified the previous day as Flat Nose Butte. Close up, the craggy height bore not the slightest resemblance to a human head. It was merely another featureless chunk of rock.

Resting against the cliff face was a pile of small boulders shaped like a pyramid, and clearly man-made.

'This proves that my uncle was here.'

Without delay, Nelson set to work. Feverishly he hurled the stones aside. Assisted by Mick Riley they had soon uncovered the small entrance to a cave. But it was barely more than three feet high and less than a foot in width.

'That uncle of your'n must have been one small dude,' observed Riley, shaking his head. They all stared at the tiny constricted entrance.

'According to Ma, Uncle Jeb was a big fella,' pointed out Nelson. 'It must have been that double-crossing partner of his who buried the stuff.'

Riley put into words what each of them was thinking. 'Ain't no way either of us can get in there.'

Nelson scratched his head in despair. All this way just to be balked at the final hurdle. If only he'd thought to bring a couple of sticks of dynamite. He kicked a rock in futile impotence.

That was when Chen Shing came to their rescue.

'Little man have many uses denied to giant. Squeeze through there easy.'

Nelson had forgotten about the Chinaman. His eyes lit up. A new hope registered on the taut visage. He recalled Chen Shing's previous handiness in tight corners.

The little fellow slid off the back of the *burro*, waddled across to the constricted entrance to the hoard of gold and peered into the black maw. He winked at Nelson who handed him a lighted torch. Then he crammed his misshapen frame through the narrow gap and disappeared from view.

Two minutes passed.

'Can you see anything?' Nelson's tense shout echoed back through the gap.

The reply that greeted his enquiry propelled slivers of ice down his spine. A terrifying scream rent the thick air, blood-curdling in its intensity. Before any of them had chance to think, another tortured screech assailed their ears.

Nelson stuck his head through the narrow gap. At the far side of the small chamber, he could see the torch brand. Jammed into a crack, its flickering illumination, though weak and vaporous, was enough to reveal the macabre tableau in all its gruesome detail.

Nelson was stunned into silence. His heart pounded against his ribcage.

At least twenty snakes were angrily striking at this intruder into their domain. Chen Shing must have disturbed their nest and the loathsome creatures had taken umbrage in time-honoured fashion. Intermingled with the Chinaman's rapidly weakening cries were the staccato rattle of tail bones. A mesmerizing if ghastly scenario, hypnotic in its repulsiveness.

Yet even through all this horror, Nelson could clearly see his Uncle Jeb's legacy – five bags in total. His mind was torn between saving his partner and losing the gold.

Guilt tore at his innards for even considering the latter option.

As if from afar the panic-stricken entreaties of his partners filtered through Nelson's paralysed brain.

'What in thunderation is going on?' demanded Riley, tugging at Nelson's shirt.

'Is he hurt?' came the more distressed question from the girl.

The young man shook himself. Then he withdrew his head from the grisly tomb.

'Chen's disturbed a rattlers' nest,' he gasped out. 'It was terrible. Like a vision from Hell. I saw three full-grown critters burying their poison packers in his body. And there were a heck of a lot more on the prod.' Then, as if to show that he had not lost his sense of their purpose, he added, 'But the gold is in there.'

Tears ran down his cheeks even as he voiced the damning remark.

'This is no time for shilly-shallying,' said Emma brusquely. 'We have to get him out of there, and quick!'

'How?'

'I'm small enough to squeeze through that gap.' Even as she spoke, Emma was taking off her coat and moving towards the narrow crack.

'You can't do that,' blustered Nelson. The thought of this lovely creature placing herself in such danger appalled him.

'You'll never be getting through that wee hole.' Riley's concurrence pressed a more practical aspect for the girl's consideration.

She ignored them both.

Before either could restrain her, Emma was wriggling through the gap. It was an extrememly tight squeeze. Elbows and knees chafed against the sharp rock, leaving red streaks where the flesh had been torn. For one brief moment, she hung there, half-in, half-out. Caught between a rock and a hard place. But she was not giving up now. One final twist and the constricted entrance to the cave had been breached.

She quickly adjusted her eyes to the shadowy gloom. A sharp intake of breath followed as she recognized that Nelson's comment regarding the chamber's likeness to the Devil's domain was no exaggeration. Emma shrugged off the shocking realization, her pragmatic nature immediately asserting itself.

She grabbed hold of the flaming brand and wafted it towards the slithering rattlers. Instantly, they backed off. But it could only be a temporary reprieve. With her other hand she dragged the Chinaman's inert form towards the cave entrance. It was lucky for her that, being a dwarf, Chen Shing was such a lightweight.

The snakes followed, their movements tentative but alert, waiting for a suitable opening to resume the attack. They lunged at Emma's flailing boots as the torch became ever weaker. Only a brief flicker remained as she reached the entrance.

'Grab his arm and heave!' she yelled.

The small body was whisked out of the cave. One final waft of the torch and Emma followed, pursued by a jarring discord of irate hissing from the thwarted reptiles. One large diamondback, foolish enough to stick its swaying head out of the cave, was quickly dispatched by the butt end of Riley's pistol.

Exerting great care, they laid Chen on his back, a rolled-up coat placed behind his large ungainly head.

Emma sucked in great lungfuls of air. She was shaking uncontrollably. The escapade had shattered the girl's nerves. Without thinking, Nelson took her in his arms and held her tightly. Gently stroking the soft tresses of her hair, he soothed the trembling frame with words of comfort.

Traces of jealousy flared for an instant in Riley's hard features. But he was not a vindictive man, and was prepared to accept the inevitable, whatever that might be. Emma would decide.

'Is-is he alive?' she stuttered out. All of them, especially Emma, had developed a warm affection for the little Chinaman.

'Hanging in there by the skin of his teeth,' replied Riley, adding in a tight whisper, 'though without the proper doctoring, I don't reckon much to his chances.'

At that moment, Chen Shing's watery eyes flickered open.

'Your uncle right after all,' he croaked gripping Nelson's arm. 'No give up on quest he sent you. Chinese proverb say, if at first not succeed, try try again.'

'I could have sworn that was Scottish,' observed

Riley, aiming a puzzled frown at the dying man.

'Chinese in there first.' For a moment Chen appeared to rally. A weak smile crossed the little fellow's drawn face. But the effort was too much. The whites of his eyes had sunk to mere pin-pricks. 'No matter. You give Chop Suey's share of gold to father. He live in St Louis.' A paroxysm of coughing followed, bubbles of red issuing from between clenched teeth. The end was nigh.

'We'll have you fixed up afore you know it,' Nelson assured him. But his words held little conviction. And Chen knew it.

'Not much time left.' He tried to pull himself upright. 'You promise to dig out gold somehow. Otherwise, wasted journey.'

All Nelson could do was give a brief nod of accord. Emma held back the floodgates with a supreme effort of will.

'One thing more.' Chen coughed up a globule of blood, his dull eyes seeking out the Irishman. 'Nelson and me got nicknames. What your's?'

Riley's face assumed the colour of a raging sunset as the others focused on him. It was something on which Nelson had often pondered, but never got around to asking.

They waited.

Slowly, the big fellow pointed to his hair that glimmered in the early sunlight.

'Carrots.' The word was uttered in little more than a whisper.

'Say again!' breathed Chen, struggling to raise himself.

'Carrots! Carrots! OK?' hollered Riley turning away to hide his embarrassment.

Nelson could barely contain a smile. Chen roared with laughter but the outburst precipitated a lethal convulsion. His twisted body quivered, then slumped back. The flat stare informed the three remaining partners that he was no more.

But at least he had gone with a smile on his face.

FOURTEEN

TRAPPED

All they could do for Chen Shing was to cover his body with rocks and mark the spot with a makeshift cross. At least it stymied the winged predators which had begun to gather on the surrounding crags.

'You reckon he was Christian?' asked Riley standing before the tiny grave, hat clutched tightly to his front.

'Don't matter none now, does it?' Nelson's shoulders lifted. Wearily, he dragged a grubby necker across his sweating brow. 'Wherever he's gone can't be worse than this God-forsaken wilderness.'

It was mid-morning. Not a cloud could be seen in the azure firmament enabling the orange globe to give full vent to its awesome fury.

'So how are we going to extract that gold from the cave?'

Nelson considered the dilemma for a while. His brow was knitted in thought.

Emma had got a fire going and was cooking some bacon. The mouth-watering aroma reminded the two men that they had not eaten a hot meal since the previous day.

It was the action of the girl pouring oil into the frying pan that gave Nelson the germ of an idea.

'How much of that stuff have we got left?'

Emma gave him a quizzical look as she moved across to the small cache of stores. After a brief rummage, the reply came back, 'Four bottles of cooking oil, and one of coal oil.'

He snapped his fingers in glee.

'That has to be our way out of this fix.'

'How do you mean?'

'We soak all our spare duds in the stuff then burn the critters out.' Nelson's initial enthusiasm for his plan was tempered by a reserved appeal to his new found love. 'It will mean you going back in there to hook out the gold. But we'll make darned certain there's none of them varmints left to bother you.'

Riley butted in with an alternative.

'If you can't bring yourself to go back in there,' he said, 'Nelson and I will quite understand. We can always come back later and blast the cave apart with dynamite.'

Emma regarded them both with a thoughtful gaze as she pondered the notion. The last thing she wanted was to return to that repellent den of torment. Riley's suggestion was appealing but would involve considerable delay. An option they could ill afford. If they were to make a success of this expedition, Nelson's plan was the only possibility.

'OK,' she said at last. 'I'll do it.'

Once the decision had been made, the meal was forgotten. A gold-hungry appetite that had occupied Horatio Muckleheimer's thoughts for so long had taken precedence.

Amassing the small bundle of clothing, they soaked the lot thoroughly in oil. Nelson leaned into the narrow aperture as far as he was able and flung the sodden bundle into the far corner. A couple of ignited brands quickly followed. Another was kept in reserve for Emma to use.

In less than a minute smoke began billowing from the cave. A loud hissing informed the fire-raisers that the rattlesnakes were none too pleased. A half-dozen emerged from the cave. Doped and lethargic from the smoke, they were immediately pounced upon and bludgeoned.

The fire continued for another half-hour before the smoke eventually dispersed. The cloying odour of burnt flesh stung his throat when Nelson stuck his head into the gap. The reserve torch lit up the interior of the chamber, revealing that its deadly occupants had all succumbed to the ferocious assault.

'All clear!' he announced handing the torch to Emma. 'But keep your eyes peeled for any lingerers.'

There was no rush this time as Emma penetrated the chamber. The sight of innumerable burnt reptiles was just as macabre as the living had been previously. And the stench was beyond belief. She slotted the torch into a crack and worked quickly, passing out the heavy bags. An overwhelming urge to quit this bestial charnel house almost found her scrambling back outside. With a supreme effort of will power, she managed to complete the grisly task.

Having at last clambered out, she retched uncontrollably, emptying her stomach into the hot sand. Nelson fed her sips of water to ease the crippling spasms.

Once she had recovered, they sat round the five bags. Just staring. Now that the final reckoning had arrived, they were wary about confronting their acquisition. It was Riley who untied the first sack and reached inside. All eyes fastened on to the slowly emerging hand and its contents.

And there was no disputing that they had indeed finally struck paydirt.

'I'll take that!'

The guttural demand cutting through the silence was like a slap in the face, a brutal shock to the system. Not for a single minute had any of them considered that others might be in the hunt for the lost gold cache. The stunning jolt was paralysing to both mind and body. They just stared at each other, uncomprehendingly.

'You hear me? Now do as I say and move away from that loot,' came the threatening demand. 'That is, if'n you don't want a bellyful of lead.'

Nelson was first to recover. He recognized that odious voice.

Five men stood in a line, some twenty yards away, holding a gun in each hand. They had made no move to come any closer. Yet even through the bleary haze of mind-numbing disappointment Nelson recognized the burly figure of Diamond Jim Garrison. And there on his left was Randy Quail, the bastard who had skewered him on the banks of the Pecos.

Riley had likewise recognized that arrogant brogue.

'Well, if it ain't Mister Garrison,' he quipped in a jovial, almost flippant tone. 'And what brings you out to this remote spot?'

The gang leader cursed. 'Don't play games with me,' he growled, irritation at the delay causing his bulbous snout to twitch. 'Just move away from the gold, nice and easy like.'

'Well, I don't think we can do that, *Mister* Garrison.' Riley's casual repartee disguised an inner turmoil, a sick feeling in his guts. He was playing for time. 'Seeing as how this here gold is the property of my partner here. Mr Horatio Muckleheimer.'

He jabbed a thumb at Nelson who was attempting to work out how these polecats had latched on to their trail. How could anyone else have known about the hidden stash?

He voiced his disquiet openly.

'Before we do anything, Garrison,' he rapped acidly, 'tell me who spilled the beans on us?'

A caustic howl of laughter erupted from a small wiry jigger standing on the far left.

'That was me, feller. Coonskin Lamaar is the name.' Nelson remained tight-lipped. He was still none the wiser. 'Your Uncle Jeb and me were partners. The old bastard thought he'd done me in. But unlike him, I came through. Now me and my new partners are here to collect. So you'd be advised to cough up afore anyone gets hurt.'

'So, it was you who knifed Uncle Jeb! And now you're after robbing me of my inheritance.' It was a statement that needed no answer.

Nevertheless, Lamaar complied. 'That's about it, boy.'

Nelson was all for hauling off there and then. Only the calming influence of Mick Riley stayed his itchy hand.

'Easy there, young Nelson' he drawled quietly. 'No way are these fellers going to let us ride out of here alive. As I see it, there's only one way out of this situation.'

'And what's that?'

'We draw our weapons together and blast away. Take them by surprise. They may cut us down, but at least this way we take some with us.' He fixed Nelson and Emma with a stoical gaze. 'What do you say?'

Emma squeezed Nelson's hand. She gave him a look as though regretting what might have been. But she recognized that there was no way out. A single tear traced a path down the young man's stubbled cheek. He nodded in agreement.

The two men were on their own. Although Emma was proficient in the use of both pistol and rifle, she had left both back at the camp.

'Keep low,' said Nelson with feeling, 'And just maybe' – he paused, a lump in his throat – 'you might come out of this in one piece.'

'If I can't be with you, I don't want to survive,' she wailed.

'Then do it to get even.' Nelson's tone was hard, brittle. 'For your father's sake.'

'How can life be so cruel,' she sobbed. 'To find love only for it to be snatched away like this. It's not fair.'

There was no answer to that. All he could offer was to take as many of the varmints with him as possible.

'It's make your mind up time, suckers,' shouted Garrison, sure in the knowledge that the gold was his for the taking. 'And your time has run out.'

Riley offered Nelson his hand. They shook.

'Ready?'

A curt nod from Nelson. 'As ever was.'

A flight of cactus wrens swooped by, completely oblivious to the violent showdown being played out below.

'Now!' yelled Riley. 'And make every shot count.'

Together, the two *amigos* snatched at their hoglegs and began blazing away. The sudden resolve to challenge Garrison's apparently unassailable position took the desperadoes by surprise.

First to experience the change in fortunes was the Arkansas Kid, who doubled over clutching at his punctured stomach. The sharp cry of anguish was enough to impel the gang into retaliatory action.

'Cut 'em down!' hollered Garrison, returning fire with both his revolvers. His curt command showed a hint of panic at being caught on the hop. 'Don't let the skunks escape now.'

Even with the Kid out of action, that still left eight guns facing two; heavy odds in anybody's book. And it was Riley who was first to suffer the overwhelming firepower. He gasped, reeling backwards as his right leg buckled. Another bullet caught him high on the left shoulder. The heavy revolver fell to the ground seconds before its owner.

Nelson was soon down to his last bullet. His first shot had been a lucky hit. A bullet plucked at his sleeve. Another ricocheted off a rock to his left. Then he felt a searing jolt of agony trace a line across his scalp. Blood trickled down his dust-caked visage. Sinking to his knees beside Emma, he grabbed hold of her outstretched hand.

Through the swirling haze of gunsmoke the hulking outline of Diamond Jim Garrison relentlessly advanced towards him. The man paused in mid-stride. He had discarded one pistol and was desperately reloading the other.

Randy Quail was lining up to finish Riley off.

Nelson aimed carefully and fired.

Nothing. Just a click. At the critical moment the weapon had jammed.

'Agh! Not now!' He screamed in frustration, then flung the useless hunk of metal at his enemy. Quail fended it off easily.

Garrison merely laughed. The ugly sound emerged as a bestial cackle echoing back off the canyon wall.

'Prepare to meet your Maker, son of a bitch,' he snarled. The reloaded gun pointed, the hammer snapping back.

Nelson closed his eyes, tensing his body for the final impact.

But it never came. Tentatively, he opened his eyes.

They bulged wide at the sight now confronting him. Garrison and his gang lay sprawled in the sand with arrows sticking out of their backs.

And there, on the crest of the dune, was a line of at least twenty mounted Indians, painted up and sporting war feathers.

Nelson could only gape at the strange apparitions.

Was he in Heaven? Or was this some ghoulish nightmare?

One of the Indians detached himself from the group and nudged his palomino down the slope. He reined up three yards in front of Nelson. He was a tribal elder and an important man judging by his upright bearing. His dried-up face was seamed and cracked like old saddle leather.

He raised his left arm in a sign of peace. 'Me Buffalo Tongue, chief of Mescalero Apache. Jeb Stockwell save life. Debt now repaid.'

'How did you know we were here?' asked Nelson, who was fast recovering from their recent brush with death.

'Big man talk too much.' With profound contempt he spat on the recumbent heap that had been Diamond Jim Garrison. Then without another word, he swung his horse and galloped away to rejoin his brothers. A single lift of his bow arm was the only acknowledgement as the line of Apaches disappeared into the wilderness.

Nelson could hardly credit the way things had turned out. From certain death, a miraculous reprieve. His eyes glassed over as he offered a silent prayer of thanksgiving.

In a daze he stumbled over to where Emma was applying a bandage to Riley's shoulder.

'How is he?' The anxious query was spoken in a hushed voice.

'I'll live, me fine young sprout,' croaked the badly mauled, but sanguine Irishman.

Nelson smiled. Glancing at Emma, he could not help feeling that life was looking distinctly more attractive.

In every possible way!